THE ORPHAN'S SILVER SPOON

Victorian Romance

FAYE GODWIN

Tica House
Publishing

Sweet Romance that Delights and Enchants!

Copyright © 2021 by Faye Godwin

All rights reserved.

No part of this book may be reproduced in any form or by any electronic or mechanical means, including information storage and retrieval systems, without written permission from the author, except for the use of brief quotations in a book review.

PERSONAL WORD FROM THE AUTHOR

Dearest Readers,

I'm so delighted that you have chosen one of my books to read. I am proud to be a part of the team of writers at Tica House Publishing. Our goal is to inspire, entertain, and give you many hours of reading pleasure. Your kind words and loving readership are deeply appreciated.

I would like to personally invite you to sign up for updates and to become part of our **Exclusive Reader Club**—it's completely Free to Join! I'd love to welcome you!

Much love,

Faye Godwin

FAYE GODWIN

CLICK HERE to Join our Reader's Club and to Receive Tica House Updates!

https://victorian.subscribemenow.com/

CONTENTS

Personal Word From The Author   1

PART I
Chapter 1   7
Chapter 2   13
Chapter 3   23
Chapter 4   30
Chapter 5   43
Chapter 6   52

PART II
Chapter 7   65
Chapter 8   78
Chapter 9   87

PART III
Chapter 10   99
Chapter 11   107
Chapter 12   115
Chapter 13   127

PART IV
Chapter 14   135
Chapter 15   147
Chapter 16   155
Chapter 17   161
Chapter 18   168
Chapter 19   177
Chapter 20   183
Chapter 21   193

Chapter 22	197
Chapter 23	206
Epilogue	211
Continue Reading...	216
Thanks For Reading	219
More Faye Godwin Victorian Romances!	221
About the Author	223

PART I

CHAPTER 1

Doxie was crying again.

Or perhaps she was crying still; crying was a common thread that ran through all her days, from the mornings when she woke in the hard bunk she shared with three other little girls under a tattered blanket, to the evenings when they sat in long rows and ate gruel for supper. There was so much cold, and she was so often hungry, and there were times when weeping felt like the only way to keep from exploding from the sheer misery of it all.

But right now, it was different from the usual sniffle over feeling cold or hungry or tired or hurt. This was a gut-wrenching sob, something deep and inconsolable that bubbled up from the very pit of Doxie's belly and threatened to tear her throat in pieces each time it burst to the surface.

She had her knees drawn up to her chest, her cheek pressed against her patched skirt, her arms wrapped around her head. Even though she was already hiding in the closet, she felt she could never hide well enough. She could never escape far enough from the pain of this world.

When the soft knock came to the door of the closet, Doxie didn't know whether she was dismayed or a little relieved. Perhaps some corner of her had wanted to be found, after all. She held back her sobs but said nothing.

"Doxie?" The voice was warm and welcome. "Can I come in, darling?"

Doxie lifted her head. "Miss Claire," she choked out, and allowed the sobs to take her again.

The closet door opened. Any other matron in the orphanage would have grabbed Doxie by the ear and hauled her out into the daylight, but Miss Claire, as always, seemed to understand. She sat down in the doorway of the closet, smoothing down her own oft-mended skirt as she looked at Doxie.

"Now, now, child," she said gently. "What's all this blubber about, then?"

Doxie covered her face with her hands and sobbed louder.

"Come on, pet." Miss Claire moved a little closer. "You know you can tell me." Her soft accent lilted as she spoke. "Did you scribble on your slate again and get caned?"

"No," sobbed Doxie.

"Good, because you're seven years old, and you know better," said Miss Claire. "So tell me, what is it?"

Doxie bit her lip. "It's Josie," she said.

"Josie?" Miss Claire sighed. "What did she tell you this time?"

"She told me that I was nobody," said Doxie. "That I was only a little more than a ghost. That no one knows me, or cares about me, or even knows where I'm from." She began to sob again. "She told me that my mama left me on the doorstep because I was too ugly to live."

"Oh, pet, that's just not true," said Miss Claire.

"But maybe she did, Miss Claire," said Doxie. "Maybe Mama hated me. Why else would she leave a baby all on her own in the cold? She must have hated me so much. I don't know why."

"Oh, Doxie." Miss Claire reached for her, took her thin arms in her gentle hands, tugged her into her soft lap. She stroked Doxie's hair; the touch was a little unfamiliar, but Doxie found herself leaning into it, burying her head in Miss Claire's chest as she cried.

Crying into someone's arms and crying alone in a closet were two very different things, Doxie was learning. But neither could entirely relieve the terrible, crushing feeling in her chest, that maybe it was true: maybe she had been left here, in this place of cold and hunger, because even as a baby she was too unacceptable to keep.

"It's not true, my love. Your mama didn't hate you," said Miss Claire.

"How do you know?" Doxie sobbed.

Miss Claire sighed. "Can you keep a secret?"

Doxie looked up at her, curiosity jolting her out of despair. "A secret?"

"Yes."

"I can," said Doxie solemnly.

"Well, I have one for you," said Miss Claire, "but you must promise to never, ever tell the other children – or the other matrons, for that matter, or it will get taken away from you and sold."

"What will?" asked Doxie.

"Promise me first," said Miss Claire.

Doxie stared up at her. "I promise," she whispered.

Miss Claire shifted her weight, sliding a hand into the pocket of her apron. She drew forth something small and slender, something that glittered a little in the faint sunlight coming in through the dormitory window, filtered by the bare branches of the tree outside.

"Here," she said.

Doxie took it. It was a spoon; tarnished, to be sure, but gleaming more brightly than anything she'd ever seen before. There was a design on the end of the handle. She held it closer to her face, rubbing at it. It looked like a rose of some kind, twisted around something with a blade.

"A spoon?" she whispered.

Miss Claire wrapped her arms around Doxie and kissed the top of her head. "It was with you when you were brought here," she said, "tucked in the folds of the blanket you were wrapped in. Mrs. Boggs took it away, of course."

Doxie wasn't surprised. Mrs. Boggs, the head matron, always wanted everything for herself.

"I saw it then, and I thought that was the end of it – she'd sell it for sure," said Miss Claire. "But the other day, she asked me to bring her something from her desk, and when I opened the drawer – there it was. It was under some old papers; it must have gotten lost in there, and she'd forgotten about it. A little miracle, if you will."

"A miracle?" Doxie breathed. She ran her hands over the spoon, feeling as though she had been given something very precious. It was a connection to her lost past, to a family she had never known.

"Do you see now, pet?" said Miss Claire. "Your mama didn't hate you. If she did, she would never have left that with you.

She may have been very poor, and that spoon may have been the only valuable thing she had. She left it with you because she wanted you to know she loved you."

She gave Doxie a warm hug. "I think that if your mama had been able to keep you, she would have done it. I think she wanted you very much."

Doxie looked down at the small, shining object in her hands, and knew in her heart she had to do whatever it took to protect it. That spoon was her proof that someone in the world really did want her – her hope. It was the only thing she had that indicated she'd had a family once, like the children she saw walking by on the street outside the orphanage, children with smiling faces and laughing parents.

Maybe her mama would come for her one day, when she wasn't so poor anymore. Doxie closed her hands around the spoon.

As long as she could hold on to this spoon, she could hold on to that hope.

CHAPTER 2

Two Years Later

THE BUCKET WAS a little too big for Doxie to carry, but as she stumbled out of the scullery with both hands clutching the cold metal handle, neither of the two women busy cooking supper paid her any attention. She could only fill the bucket to half full, or everything would slop out on the floor as she tried to carry it. It swung wildly in her hands, and even though she tried her best not to let her knees bump against the bucket, it inevitably happened.

Panting, gritting her teeth, Doxie marched down the hallway to where she'd set the mop at the dining room door. Her arms burned; her bare feet slapped on the cold stone floor. She stumbled a little, and an arc of water splashed up out of the bucket, sloshing icily over her dress.

Doxie let out a groan of dismay. Now she'd be damp for the rest of the day; hardly any light came into the orphanage, and even on a summer's day like this one, it was cold and dark inside. There was no chance of going outside into the courtyard, either. Now it would be chores until supper, and then straight to bed.

She had finally reached the place where she'd left the mop. Setting down the bucket with a bump, she spilled some more water on the floor. Well, at least it was in the right place now. She picked up the mop and plunged it into the water, swilling it around.

Outside, she could hear a little laughter from the younger children as they played in the courtyard. It made her smile as she began to work the mop across the dirty floor. There were few things, despite the laughter of those children, that could make her smile anymore these days.

She paused to stare out of the dining room window for a few moments. There were twenty-seven other children in the orphanage, and while sixteen of them were already hard at work like her, the others were all still very small. They were playing in the courtyard, or at least, spending time outside in the courtyard; only a few of them were really playing. Somehow it was the smallest ones that seemed the most immune to the cold and hunger that gripped every day inside this dark place. They were chasing one another around the trunk of the old tree that stretched its roots down into the dust and somehow survived where every other plant had withered and died. The older children sat around in listless groups, soaking in as much sunshine as they could.

Doxie sighed. She knew she could make them all laugh and smile, if she could only go out there and play with them.

"Oi, Doxie!" barked a voice from the kitchen. "You'll never get it done if you stand about like that. Get to work!"

"Yes, ma'am," Doxie said, jumping back into action. She knew the penalty for insubordination would be a thorough spanking with her own mop if she was lucky; if she was unlucky, she'd be sent to bed without any supper. The idea was unthinkable. She got to work despite the growing sting in her heart.

Miss Claire would never have shouted at her like that. Miss Claire wouldn't be lollygagging about in the kitchen now either; she would be out there with the children, playing with them, making them laugh despite their hunger.

But Miss Claire had been gone for a whole year. And now the spoon, tucked safely in Doxie's pocket and bumping reassuringly against her leg with every movement, held even more importance for her.

It wasn't unusual for quiet sobbing to wake Doxie in the middle of the night.

In fact, this was the third night in a row that someone's crying had woken her. She lay on her hard, narrow bunk, her arms wrapped around one of the smaller girls, listening. The girl in her arms – little Mamie – was lying very still and quiet, her breathing deep and regular.

It had to be someone else who was doing the crying. Doxie sat up slowly, peering around the packed dormitory by the sliver of moonlight coming in through the single square window. There were thirteen girls crammed into the six beds of this dormitory, and it was hard to puzzle out which one it was who was crying.

It took Doxie a few moments to spot her. It was little Trudy, a tiny girl with long dark hair and luminous eyes, who slept in the bunk at the back of the room. She wasn't in her bunk now, though. She was sitting by the doorway, her head in her thin hands, weeping.

Doxie got up, tucking the blanket tightly back around Mamie, and went over to the little girl.

"What's the matter, Trudy?" she asked softly. "Have you had another bad dream?"

Trudy raised her pale little face from where she had cradled it in her arms. In the faint light, tears made white streaks through the grime on her cheeks, and her eyes were very red.

"Yes," she whispered.

Doxie sat down on the cold floor beside Trudy, wrapping an arm around the little child. Her shoulders were bony and hard to the touch.

"I dreamed of the fire again," whispered Trudy.

Doxie looked down at her, her heart breaking as the moonlight touched Trudy's left ear. It was misshapen, the skin waxy and mottled; a scar that remained after a terrible burn wound that Trudy had suffered in the fire that had taken her parents and siblings.

"I'm sorry," said Doxie, hugging her tight.

Trudy looked up at her, tears rolling down her cheeks. "I can't forget it, Doxie," she whispered. "I can't forget the way they screamed."

Her words sent icy chills down Doxie's spine. She took a deep breath, trying to think of a way to make Trudy feel better. "Would you like to hear a story?" she asked.

"Is it a happy story?" asked Trudy.

"Yes, very happy," said Doxie.

Trudy looked away. "No," she said. "I know my story will never be happy like the nice ones you tell, Doxie."

Doxie swallowed to hide her heartbreak. "How about a song, then?" she asked tremulously.

"Yes... yes." Trudy let out a sigh, nestling tightly against Doxie. "I think I'd like that."

Doxie didn't know many songs. The children were not taken to church; Mrs. Boggs read the Bible to them in the evenings, but she didn't sing. Still, once an older orphan had been brought to the orphanage, a girl who'd had a home and friends once. She had taught Doxie the words of the only song she really knew. It had a haunting familiarity to it that made Doxie feel happy and sad at the same time when she heard it.

She cradled Doxie close, keeping her voice soft as she sang it.

"Mid pleasures and palaces though we may roam, be it ever so humble, there's no place like home," she sang softly. "A charm from the skies seems to hallow us there, which seek thro' the world, is ne'er met elsewhere."

Trudy's breathing grew slow and deep, and her little head lay on Doxie's shoulder. She sang the refrain slowly, haltingly, gazing up at the moonlit window where she sat on the cold floor, hunger gnawing at her stomach.

"Home! Home! Sweet, sweet home! There's no place like home! There's no place like home!"

***

Doxie's stomach growled quietly as she worked her broom across the flagstones of the kitchen floor. The morning's porridge was bubbling on the coal stove, and even though its smell was plain and ordinary, it made her mouth water. Perhaps there would even be a little milk with her porridge this morning. Sugar was far too much to hope for; Doxie had barely tasted it in all of her life.

Still, a bellyful of porridge would get her through the day, and Doxie was glad to smell its homely and reassuring aroma as she worked.

The kitchen was her favorite place in the orphanage. It was directly behind the dining room, with the boys' dormitory on the left and the girls' dormitory on the right. The dining room looked out onto the courtyard, but the kitchen looked out into the stable yard where an ancient horse, a bony cow, a pig, and a handful of chickens made their home. The back door was open to let the summer breeze into the kitchen, and it was filled with light and air. Mrs. Boggs always complained about the smell of the hay and animals outside, but Doxie liked it. She took deep breaths of the fresh air as she swept.

There was a soft tap on the doorframe. "Egg delivery!" said a playful young voice.

Doxie's heart flipped over. This was her favorite part of every day. Straightening from her work, she turned to smile at the boy who stood in the doorway, holding a basket of fresh eggs.

"Good morning, Owen," she said, smiling.

She didn't know exactly why Owen's smile was so special to her. He was missing a bottom tooth, and truth be told, all of his teeth were spectacularly crooked; yet his smile split his face from end to end and lit up his bright blue eyes so that they danced like a summer sky on a windy day.

"Good morning!" he said, his voice lilting. He always sounded like he might just be about to break into song. "How are you this morning?"

"I'm very well, thank you." Doxie went over to him and took the basket; four little eggs lay in the bottom. "Did you sleep well?"

"You know how I love the loft." Owen laughed. "The hay makes for a much better bed than the dormitory's bunks, and I prefer the sound of old Captain moving around in his stable underneath me to the snoring of other little boys."

Doxie smiled. "That does sound good," she said.

"And how about you?" asked Owen.

"Oh, not so well." Doxie sighed. "Trudy had a dream about the fire again."

"Poor Trudy." Owen's face fell. "I can't imagine seeing… something like that. Perhaps it's a good thing that we were both abandoned."

Doxie nodded. Like her, Owen had been brought to the orphanage as a baby, left on the doorstep for Mrs. Boggs to find – only he had come two years before Doxie did. She forced a smile for him. "I miss having you here," she said, "even if you like the loft better."

"Oh, I miss playing with you and the others too." Owen shrugged. "But at least I get to see you when I bring in the eggs."

Doxie nodded. She was about to speak when she heard footsteps in the hallway and backed away from the doors. "Mrs. Boggs is coming," she said. "You'd best be going, or we'll both be in trouble for standing here talking."

"You're right. I'll be off." Owen flashed her a smile. "Have a good day, Doxie. See you tomorrow."

He said those same words to her every morning, and every morning she clung to the hope that they would be true – but she wasn't sure if they would. The truth was that, at eleven years old, Owen was about to age out of the orphanage. He was a strong boy and willing; and while he was useful enough to Mrs. Boggs now as he tended the animals, she didn't know when the matron would decide that he would be far more useful if she sold him to a chimney sweep or a blacksmith as an apprentice, or to a housekeeper as a stable boy.

A shudder ran down her spine as she stepped back and turned away to put the eggs in their place. She had already lost so much when Miss Claire died.

She wasn't sure she could handle it if she lost Owen, too.

As always, for comfort, she plunged her hand into the pocket of her apron and found the smooth, hard shape of the silver spoon. She rubbed her thumb along the edge of it, an action that had turned its tarnished surface back to bright silver as surely as if she had polished it.

At least she would never lose the knowledge that there had been one person in the world who loved her.

CHAPTER 3

THE STEADY SHRILLNESS of a baby's cry had been echoing through the orphanage all morning. Doxie gritted her teeth as she knelt in front of the kitchen grate, rubbing blacking over the iron surface. That baby had been crying for hours, almost without a pause; it had gone from a deafening shriek to a quieter, more desperate wail, hoarse and worn out, as though the infant itself had almost spent the last of its voice and its strength.

She tried to close her ears to its screaming. Miss Peggy, the young matron who had been hired in Miss Claire's place, was tending to the baby. She had been trying to calm its cries all morning, but she wouldn't succeed – even though Miss Claire would have soothed that child in moments. Miss Peggy was terrible with children. She had cold, hard, knobby hands, and cold, hard, grey eyes, and her voice was nasal and annoying.

It was difficult to ignore the baby's cries, even though Doxie knew the child was being tended to. She forced herself to concentrate on the task at hand, nonetheless. If she didn't finish polishing this grate, mopping the floor, and washing the dishes before lunchtime, she was likely to get a cane across the palm from Mrs. Boggs.

The baby went on crying until she had finished polishing, and Doxie was busy retrieving her mop and bucket from the broom cupboard when she finally heard the familiar click-clack of Mrs. Boggs walking down the hallway toward the nursery, which was next to the boys' dormitory.

"Margaret!" she bellowed. "What is going on with that baby? All that crying is giving me a horrendous headache."

Doxie shut the door of the broom cupboard and crept to the kitchen door, peering down the hallway to the nursery. Miss Peggy was standing in the doorway, the screaming infant clutched in her hands. She held the baby upright, facing away from her; Doxie could see its little face, all crumpled and blotchy with screaming, and its thin arms extended toward Mrs. Boggs.

"I pay you to take care of the children," barked Mrs. Boggs. "Why can't you seem to master the simplest task of quieting a baby?"

"I've tried everything, ma'am," snapped Miss Peggy defensively. "I've changed its nappy, I've bathed it, I've even fed it a little extra. There's something wrong with it."

As she spoke, Doxie crept up the hall toward the nursery, her eyes fixed on that poor little screaming baby boy.

"There's nothing wrong with the child, Margaret," said Mrs. Boggs impatiently. "You just can't quiet it."

The baby let out a particularly shrill squeal, and Mrs. Boggs clapped her hands over her ears. "Silence that child!" she shouted.

"Please, ma'am." Doxie had now reached Mrs. Boggs' elbow. "Please, let me try."

"You should be mopping the floor, child," said Miss Peggy angrily.

Mrs. Boggs sighed. "Just give her the baby," she said. "Anything to make it be quiet."

Miss Peggy shot Doxie a furious look, but nonetheless, she thrust the little one into Doxie's arms. Doxie wrapped her arms around him. He was so light, and so thin, swaddled in a tatty little blanket. She brought him close to her chest and started to rock gently from side to side.

Immediately, the baby's cries grew a little quieter.

"Mid pleasures and palaces though we may roam," Doxie began to sing softly. "Be it ever so humble, there's no place like home…"

As she sang, the baby's cries grew slower, softer. As she reached the end of the first stanza, he was only giving the odd little hiccup of sorrow. She stopped, tracing a finger over his soft cheek. The baby looked up at her with red eyes, but a smile was playing around his toothless little mouth. He reached up toward her face, clutching at a strand of her brown hair.

"Now see," said Mrs. Boggs angrily. "Was that so hard?"

She turned and strode off back toward her study. Miss Peggy gave Doxie another glare, but dared not say anything, turning instead to go into the nursery.

The baby gave a little whimper. Doxie leaned down and kissed the tip of his little nose. She didn't know the second stanza of the song, but she had made up more words; one stanza was never enough to lull a baby to sleep.

And though we've never had a place of our own

we hope that someday we'll all have a home.

A place where we're warm and the fire burns bright;

a place where we're safe and cozy at night.

Home! Home! Sweet home!

There's no place like home! There's no place like home!

She whispered the last words into the little baby's ear. His eyes fluttered closed, and his breathing grew deep and regular as he drifted into sleep.

THE FIRST THING that Doxie noticed about Owen the next morning was his smile. It was as beautiful as ever, but today there seemed to be an extra note of joy in it; his eyes were as bright and sparkling as the surface of the Thames on a clear summer day.

Doxie couldn't help but grin at the sight of it. "Good morning!" she said, holding out her hands.

Owen placed the egg basket in them. "Hello, Doxie," he said, almost singing the words. "How was your day?"

"Good, but maybe not as good as yours." Doxie laughed. "Why are you so happy today?"

"Well, you know old Cob?" said Owen.

Doxie nodded. She had seen how Owen fussed over the stocky little horse that pulled the orphanage's cart and carried sacks of flour back from the market. He was ancient, his once-brown coat flecked with grey, his face nearly white.

"Mrs. Boggs told me yesterday that she wanted to sell him for dog meat," said Owen. "He's so old and slow, and it's not fair for his poor old legs to keep doing the work anymore."

"Oh, no!" Doxie gasped. "Owen, that's awful."

"It would have been, if it had happened." Owen grinned. "But I was driving him home after taking away the muck yesterday afternoon when I passed by a little girl at a nice house, riding a very fiery pony that was running off with her. I put old Cob in the driveway, quick like, and the horse stopped. Her father came running out and said how much he regretted buying that fiery animal for his daughter, and well, I said that if he could pay more than the knacker man, he could buy Cob."

"And did he?" gasped Doxie.

"Yes! He did. He knew the old boy would take good care of his daughter." Owen laughed. "Doxie, I'm so relieved."

"It's a good thing you said something," said Doxie. "Or poor old Cob would be dog's meat."

"It's the least I could do for the old fellow," said Owen. "And the man paid a good price for him. Now we're going to get a new pony – something younger and stronger. Maybe we'll even be able to hire him out sometimes and make some extra money. Then we could all have more food."

"I'm glad to hear it." Doxie didn't believe it would happen; if Mrs. Boggs made more money, the children would see none of it. She smiled at Owen anyway, sadness creeping into her heart. "I hope you get apprenticed as a stable boy or a farrier when you leave," she said softly.

"Doxie." Owen reached forward, touching her hands where they held the basket. "Why are you talking like this? I'm not leaving."

"Of course, you are," Doxie mumbled, her head hanging. "You're eleven. It won't be long before you're apprenticed."

She felt Owen's hands shudder on her own. "I'm useful here," he said.

Doxie lifted her face to his. "I'll just miss you," she said quietly. "I... I love all the children here. But you're my special friend."

He looked away, a blush rising to his cheeks. "And... you too," he mumbled. "But I have a lot of work to do." He glanced at her shyly. "See you tomorrow?"

She returned his smile. "Tomorrow," she said. As he walked away, she added the words silently, deep in her heart. *I hope*.

CHAPTER 4

EVERY MORNING, while the entire orphanage lay dark and silent and asleep, it was Doxie's work to get up first and light the fires – one in the dining room, one in Mrs. Boggs' study, one in the nursery, and one in the kitchen. There were no fires in the dormitories themselves, and even though it was summer, Doxie shivered as she climbed out of bed and stood barefoot on the stone floor. It was as though the night had sucked every memory of sunlight from the room, and Doxie groped her way to where her shoes stood at the end of the bed. She pulled them on first, then changed from her nightgown into her ragged buttercup-yellow dress, pulled a holey jersey over her head and walked out of the dormitory into the dark hallway.

Owen had set the fires last night, while Doxie was helping to get the other girls ready for bed. She had flashed him a quick smile when she'd opened the door to take the dirty clothes to the scullery, but there was no time to talk; there seldom was. Still, the smile they exchanged meant more to her than many a conversation with someone else ever could.

The matchbox was in the kitchen. Doxie passed through the dining room, heading toward it, but as she passed the front door, she thought she heard something. It was something faint and feeble. Perhaps she was imagining it.

Doxie stood motionless, listening. Her heart sank at the thought of what it could be.

The sound came again. She tried to tell herself that it was just the whimper of some unhappy stray animal, or the cry of a strange bird in the branches of the old tree. But the sound that came from the direction of the courtyard had a familiarity to it that chilled her to the bone.

She would have to go and see, no matter how much she feared what she might find.

Hurrying into the kitchen, Doxie felt in a niche for a stub of candle. Mrs. Boggs never allowed the children to carry candles, but Doxie didn't have the courage to walk to the gate at the far end of the courtyard in complete darkness.

She found the matchbox on the mantelpiece. The match flared in the darkness, and in a few seconds, warm candlelight flooded the kitchen. Doxie could only hope the flicker of candlelight wouldn't wake Mrs. Boggs. Maybe she would think Doxie had just lit an uncommonly good fire.

Shielding the candle with one hand, Doxie hurried across the dining room to the front door. The keys hung on a hook by the door, just far enough that the smaller children couldn't reach it; Doxie had to stand on tiptoe. She unlocked the door and stepped out into a dark, nippy morning.

The candle flame guttered in the breeze. Doxie shivered, straining her ears to listen.

The cry came again, and this time it was unmistakable. It was the desperate, thin wail of a baby that had been abandoned; a hungry, weak baby, perhaps on the brink of death.

"I'm coming, little one!" Doxie gasped. Ignoring the sputter of the candle, Doxie ran across the courtyard, her footsteps slapping on the hard-packed earth. She reached the orphanage gate and crouched down, holding the candle out in front of her.

The sight was all too familiar. A tiny bundle of rags lay at the feet of the gate. The rags were so mismatched and filthy that Doxie might have assumed they had been discarded like the garbage they were, but the cry came up from within them, and when Doxie leaned closer, the candlelight flickered over a tiny, pale face, tinted blue with cold.

"Oh, no," Doxie gasped. The child's cries were coming more slowly and weakly now. She knew that this little one didn't have long.

She had no key for the front gate of the orphanage; Mrs. Boggs feared that the children would escape the awful place if they had the chance. Still, it hadn't stopped her from retrieving a string of other babies from outside the gate, and it wouldn't stop her this time.

Setting the candle down on the ground and kicking off her boots, Doxie reached up to grip the iron bars of the orphanage gate. Her feet found a foothold on the stone gatepost, her toes digging in between two large stones, mortar crumbling at her touch. With a grunt of effort, she scrambled over the gate and landed with a thump beside the baby.

"It's all right, little one," Doxie gasped. "I'm here."

She reached out and gathered the baby into her arms and lap, cuddling it close with her entire body in an effort to warm it. It was so very small. Looking down at its face, the features still stubby and indistinct as though they'd been roughly pressed from clay, Doxie knew the baby couldn't be more than a few days old. Perhaps even younger. She touched its cheek with her finger, and the baby turned its head hungrily, its puckered lips seeking nourishment.

"At least you're still strong enough to try," Doxie whispered. There had been times when she had lifted infants from this cold pavement to find their rags stiff with frost and dusted with snow; times when she had doubted they lived at all, until she had slipped a hand inside the rags and felt the frantic flutter of a newborn heart fighting for survival.

At other times, she had not felt that flutter. Only a cold stillness that appalled her.

"Come on." Doxie leaned down and kissed the little forehead. "There's some warm milk inside."

The baby gave another squall as Doxie scaled the fence again. The infant was small enough that she could keep it clutched under her arm as she climbed. She held on tightly, careful not to drop it, but every jostle made the baby scream more loudly. Doxie shushed it, trying not to wake the matron. She didn't need Mrs. Boggs to wake in a bad mood again.

As she swung her leg over the fence and started to climb down the gatepost, there was a loud clatter. Startled, Doxie looked down. Something had fallen out of the baby's rags; something small and square and hard.

"Now what could that be?" Doxie murmured. Stepping down to the ground, she rocked the baby a little in an attempt to soothe it, then bent down to pick up the object.

To Doxie's surprise, it was a photograph. The frame was crudely made of wood; there was no glass, which was a good thing, for it would have shattered in the fall. Holding up the photograph to the candlelight, Doxie saw two smiling faces looking up at her. The woman had dark hair, and she wore a white gown just like the Queen on her wedding day. The man's hair seemed fairer; it was impossible to tell the colour of his eyes in the sepia tones of the photo, but for some reason they seemed to Doxie that they must have been bright blue. Both of them were laughing into the camera.

Doxie felt her heart squeeze with longing. "These are your parents, aren't they?" she whispered.

Uncomprehending, the baby continued to cry lustily. It didn't understand now, but Doxie knew that in a few years, this baby would begin to ask questions – questions about parents and families that no one had the answers to.

She could feel the weight of the silver spoon in her apron pocket. She would give anything to know what her mama's smile had looked like, what colour her papa's hair had been. She would give anything, anything in the world – except perhaps her friendship with Owen – to see a photograph of her two parents.

"Doxie?" shouted a voice from the doorway. "What baby is that?"

Doxie whirled around, instinct taking over her movements. She shoved the photograph down her apron pocket before she could think, and her heart skipped a beat. Mrs. Boggs would want to take that photo away from her and sell it, she knew it. But she couldn't let this baby lose the only link it had to its past.

But it wasn't Mrs. Boggs in the doorway. It was Miss Peggy, and she was watching Doxie with her usual suspicion. Her eyes flashed to Doxie's pocket, and for a terrible moment, she feared the young matron would ask her what she had put in there.

Before Miss Peggy could say anything, Doxie spoke. "I found it crying outside, Miss Peggy," she said. "Someone must have left it here."

Miss Peggy sighed. "Not again." She shook her head. "Come on. You'd best bring it inside."

Doxie clutched the baby close to her chest and hurried into the orphanage. With every step she took, the photograph bumped against her legs.

WHEN DOXIE ROSE the next morning, the baby girl she had found outside the day before was still sleeping peacefully. She had cried so much of the day yesterday; no matter how much milk Doxie fed her, the little one never seemed satiated; no matter how long she had sat by the fire with her, the tiny hands and feet never quite felt warm. Miss Peggy had taken her a few times, but each time Mrs. Boggs would shout at her to give the baby back to Doxie; she simply wouldn't quiet in Miss Peggy's arms.

It had been late last night, as Doxie cuddled the baby in her bunk with her, that the little one finally fell asleep. Now, as Doxie rose to light the fires and gathered the baby in her ragged blanket, the child barely stirred. At first, Doxie felt a pang of fear as she carried the baby into the kitchen. But when she struck the match and held the wobbling flame over the baby's face, it was pink and unlined, the little eyes closed, the breaths calm.

"You're safe now," Doxie whispered, running the back of a finger over the baby's forehead. She stirred a little but did not wake.

Doxie carried the baby with her into the nursery and laid her in a crib with two others before lighting the fire there. Then she lit the one in the dining room, and finally, headed to Mrs. Boggs' study. But as she approached the room, she saw the flicker of light coming from under the door.

Sometimes Mrs. Boggs rose early. Often, however, her early mornings spelled trouble. Doxie felt deep cold in the pit of her belly. She thought of the photograph of the baby's parents. She had hidden it under her pillow at the first opportunity yesterday; it clinked against the spoon in her pocket when she walked, and she didn't want to be found out.

Had someone found her out anyway?

Taking a deep breath, Doxie walked up to the door of the study, knowing that if she didn't check on the fire, she would be in trouble anyway. She raised her fist and tapped twice on the peeling paint.

"It's me, ma'am," she said nervously. "I just want to check on the fire."

"Come in," snapped Mrs. Boggs.

She already sounded like she was in a bad mood. Steeling herself for angry glares and snappish criticisms, Doxie gripped the matches tightly, took a deep breath, and pushed the door open.

There was nothing wrong with the fire. It leaped high behind the grate, crackling merrily and filling the study with golden light. The study itself was one of the few rooms in the orphanage that had any form of luxury; there was a rug on the floor and a painting of green fields and blue skies on the wall, and Doxie polished Mrs. Boggs' oak desk twice a week.

Still, this time, she didn't revel in the comfort of the room. Instead, a pang of fear ran her through. Why hadn't Mrs. Boggs simply told her that the fire needed no tending?

The door slammed behind her. Doxie jumped, spinning around, a spray of matches scattering out of the box. Miss Peggy stood by the door, her eyes glittering as she folded her arms. There was a look of triumph in them – a look that frightened Doxie to the bone.

There was a click from the direction of the desk. Doxie turned slowly, her heart pounding in her chest. Mrs. Boggs had placed something on the polished surface: something small and square and hard.

Her eyes were black with menace. "Do you care to explain yourself, you lazy, thieving child?" she growled.

Doxie swallowed hard and took a step closer to the desk. The fact that Mrs. Boggs had said nothing about the matches terrified her; it meant that the matron was truly irate. She looked down into the wide smiles and laughing eyes of the baby's parents on their wedding day.

"Miss Peggy thought she saw you putting something in your pocket yesterday morning," said Mrs. Boggs. "She told me, but I thought she was imagining things. I never thought you, of all the children here, would dare to steal from me." Her eyes narrowed. "But I gave her permission to search the dormitory nonetheless, while you were bathing that new baby, and she found this under your pillow."

Doxie swallowed hard, looking up into Mrs. Boggs' eyes. "I was afraid that..." she began, then stopped.

"You found it with the new baby, didn't you?" said Mrs. Boggs.

Doxie dropped her gaze. "Yes," she said softly.

"Then why didn't you turn it over to me?" Mrs. Boggs snapped. "You know that anything you bring through those gates is my property – mine alone. Including you."

Doxie felt a tear run, hot and silent, down her cheek. She knew that there was nothing she could say to Mrs. Boggs that would change the matron's mind, no matter how certain Doxie was that the only theft that had been committed was the theft of that photograph from that helpless little baby.

"I wanted her to know what her parents looked like," Doxie whispered.

"Her parents?" Mrs. Boggs rose from her seat, slamming her hands down on the desk. "Her parents! As if they were important in any way!" she thundered. "Her *parents* are the ones who gave her up! Her parents are the ones who made her a burden upon me! If it wasn't for all your *parents* who keep dumping you here at the gates, I would have an easier life!"

Doxie trembled as though Mrs. Boggs' words were a lash across her shoulders. The tears came faster now, and she longed to reach into her pocket and clutch that spoon for comfort, but she dared not touch it – not here with Miss Penny and Mrs. Boggs staring at her. If they took that spoon from her, too…

They were going to take the photograph from the baby, though. They were going to rob her of the only chance she would ever have to know where she had come from.

"Please, ma'am," Doxie whispered, raising her eyes to Mrs. Boggs'. "Please, don't sell the picture. Give it to the baby when she gets big enough."

Mrs. Boggs' eyes widened in shock and utter rage. "You are a very, very bad child," she hissed. "You are an insolent, ungrateful, lazy, dishonest, treacherous rat, and I will not have you under my roof for a moment longer." She sat down heavily in her chair, as though exhausted by her own anger. "Margaret!"

"Yes, ma'am?" said Miss Peggy, shooting Doxie a victorious look.

"Get her out of this place." Mrs. Boggs turned her attention to a ledger on the desk. "Make sure she never comes back."

Absolute shock filled Doxie's veins like ice. "What?" she cried.

"You heard her, you foul little wench," snapped Miss Peggy. She seized Doxie's arm, her fingernails digging painfully into the skin. "You're not welcome here anymore."

"No!" Doxie cried, terror burning through her as she thought of the great and twisted streets surrounding the orphanage. "No! No! Please! Don't take me out there!"

Miss Peggy yanked her out of the study and slammed the door behind them. Doxie screamed and screamed, tears gushing down her cheeks, her entire body and mind consumed with total fear. But Miss Peggy ignored every cry, every desperate clawing of Doxie's free hand against her own. She dragged her out of the front door and down the long path in the dark to the gates of the orphanage courtyard. Beyond, a single streetlamp made a fruitless attempt at bringing some kind of illumination to the long street. The houses loomed around them like shadowed giants; the light showed only a few scraps of wanton poverty – a damp bit of torn newspaper fluttering in the edge of a puddle that shimmered with an oily sheen; a bone-thin, one-eyed cat, pausing to glance up at Doxie's screaming as it scuttled across the sidewalk; a discarded drink bottle, dark and cracked, lying in the gutter.

Miss Peggy shoved the gate open. With a harsh hand on Doxie's back, she shoved her bodily into the street; the push was enough to knock Doxie off her feet, and she landed heavily on her hands and knees, her scream cutting off short. When she scrambled to her feet and spun around, Miss Peggy had already slammed and locked the gate behind her.

"No!" Doxie choked out. She rushed to the gate, grasping the cold bars in her small hands and staring desperately between them at Miss Peggy. "No," she whispered. "Please. I'll die out here. I'll starve. I'll…" She stopped, overwhelmed by the looming tide of horrors waiting for her in these dark and lonely streets.

Miss Peggy tossed her head, giving Doxie one last glare.

"This is the penalty for your insolence, child," she hissed. "You brought this on yourself."

She turned around and stalked back into the orphanage, leaving Doxie alone in the world.

CHAPTER 5

As the sun rose reluctantly, dragging its feet up the long slope of the day, Doxie wrapped her arms around her cold body and wandered in the only direction she knew. There had been no time for her to take her coat. She wore only her dress and jersey, and while that was comfortable within the walls of the orphanage, the wind now sliced through the fibers and prickled her skin with a thousand icy needles. It found its way up her skirt, chilled her legs, poked long, cold fingers down the neck of her dress.

The tears drying on her cheeks grew colder with every gust of wind. As the streets turned from black to grey, Doxie's feet carried her toward the run-down marketplace near the orphanage. On days when Miss Peggy was disinclined to leave the warmth of the orphanage, she had often stopped? Doxie's hand with the meager money that Mrs. Boggs allowed for feeding the children and sent her off to the market. The people there were the only ones that Doxie knew outside of the orphanage.

Perhaps they would help her. They would *have* to help her; Doxie knew that the alternative was unthinkable. A night out here, on these streets, alone… She couldn't think of a way she would survive.

Fresh tears coursed down her cheeks as she walked into the market square, her familiar surroundings distorted by her fear and by the early hour. If only she could have spoken to Owen one last time. All this time, she had been so afraid that he was the one who was going to be taken from her. She had never thought that she would be driven out instead.

Now, she skirted around every shadow. The grotesque forms of the marketplace seemed so much more looming and dangerous so early in the morning; the rickety stalls with their bent poles and ragged roofs; the puddles of grubby water where cobblestones had gone missing from the ground. The stallholders were busy setting up their makeshift stalls, and even they looked more frightening in this light. The shadows seemed to gather in the folds and wrinkles of their old and weathered skin; what light there was, was unkind to the sores and the goiters, the circles underneath the eyes, the gnarled hands that overwork had bent and twisted like the branches of ancient oaks.

Doxie went first to the stall halfway down the market square on her left, where an old man sold slightly wilted vegetables and always managed to hold onto a little jolliness despite the rheumatism that bent him almost double. He was arranging some rather soft carrots painstakingly in a box, balanced on the plank over two barrels that he used as a table, when Doxie approached.

"M-Mr. Wainwright?" Doxie said nervously.

"Good morning, little one!" he said cheerfully, his eyes still on his carrots. "You're out buying groceries early today, aren't you?"

"No, sir." Doxie felt her voice break. "I'm not buying anything."

Mr. Wainwright looked up, surprise crossing his face, followed by shock when his eyes rested on Doxie's tear-streaked face. "Why, my dear child," he said, pushing the carrots aside and leaning over the plank, "what on earth is the matter?"

"I was – I was chased out of the orphanage, sir," she whimpered. "I found a baby outside with a little photograph in her rags, and I hid it away for her, and they said I was stealing." Fear and shame rose in her, and she covered her face with her thin hands. "I didn't mean to do anything wrong. And now I'm all alone." She wept.

"Doxie, Doxie, my child." Mr. Wainwright reached a hard old hand over the planks and patted her shoulder helplessly. "Where are you going to go?"

"I don't know." Doxie let her hands fall by her sides and looked up at him again, her heart shattered. "I need help."

Deep sorrow came to Mr. Wainwright's eyes. His habitual smile faded from his face, and he looked away. When he spoke, the bounce had left his voice; it was flat and lifeless.

"I can do nothing for you," he said heavily. "I live in a tenement with other men. You would not be safe there."

Doxie felt her hope growing smaller and smaller, like a candle flame flickering desperately in a cold draft. If anyone here would help her, she knew it was Mr. Wainwright. And if he couldn't, would there be anyone else?

"I'm sorry," said Mr. Wainwright.

Doxie heard his voice break and couldn't bear it. She couldn't see a grown man cry. Looking up, she forced a smile. "I'll be all right, Mr. Wainwright," she said. "Don't worry."

Mr. Wainwright shook his head, then leaned forward and touched her shoulder again. "Let me ask one thing of you, Doxie," he said.

"Yes, sir?" said Doxie, confused. What could she possibly do for the old fellow?

"Never lose this," he said softly, jabbing an uncomfortable old finger into the center of her chest over her heart. "Never let the world harden the soft and beautiful heart you have. Kindness is a rare thing here in London, rarer than platinum or diamonds, and far, far better. If you can have a good heart – if you can keep your good heart in a place like this – then you are a jewel, a rare and perfect jewel, no matter what any part of the world will ever tell you."

Doxie knew by the burning of Mr. Wainwright's eyes that he believed every word he was telling her, but she didn't – not one of them. She felt nothing like a jewel of any kind; she felt cold and hungry and afraid and alone, her dress was ragged, her face was dirty, and all she wanted was to find somewhere warm to sleep that night.

No, perhaps that wasn't true; all she wanted was to go back home to the orphanage and tell Owen everything. But she knew he couldn't help her. Perhaps no one could.

Mr. Wainwright sighed, as if reading her mind. "You'll understand someday," he said quietly, "God willing." He reached into the box of carrots and pulled out two of them, then took a tattered canvas bag and tucked the two carrots and a slightly wrinkled apple into it. "Take this."

"Oh, thank you, sir." Doxie grabbed the bag eagerly, relief washing over her. At least she would have something to eat today.

"Go safely, Doxie child," said Mr. Wainwright. "I hope you find somewhere warm to stay." He paused. "And if you don't, come and sleep here, under the table. It's quiet enough here at night."

Doxie shuddered at the thought. She knew there were rats in this square, and she wondered if people wandered around here – sometimes drunken and singing, sometimes sick and blank-eyed – the way they wandered up and down the street passing the orphanage.

"Thank you, sir," said Doxie, nonetheless. She glanced around the rest of the square, at the other people setting up their stalls all around it. They were all familiar faces: she had bought salt and flour from the old woman in the corner, hard cheese from the young girl with the goat, bread from the sour-faced baker. There was only one she didn't recognise – a thin creature, struggling to build a fire from damp wood, a sack of porridge oats and a large cast-iron pot standing nearby.

Doxie squared her shoulders. She'd avoid the thin woman with the pot, but she knew everyone else. Someone in this square would have to help her.

The alternative, to sleep here in Mr. Wainwright's stall, was simply unthinkable.

THE DAY WAS A LONG ONE, filled with many a hard and frightening lesson for Doxie, and it ended with exactly what she had so dreaded: crawling underneath Mr. Wainwright's stall for the night.

The first lesson she had learned was that an apple and two carrots looked like enough food for the whole day, but when one was very hungry and unaccustomed to having the whole day's food given to one at breakfast, they could vanish very quickly. Doxie nibbled away the first carrot within ten minutes, and tried to save the second, but the morning was chilly, and she had walked a long way in the cold. The second carrot disappeared shortly thereafter, and bite by bite through the course of the morning, so did the apple.

By midday, she had learned her second lesson, and this one was far more heartbreaking: that most people were kind and helpful only if one was giving them money. She had thought that everyone in the market square was basically kind, nice, and decent, but previously when she had interacted with them, she had been buying things from them. The sour-faced baker always used to give her something of a smile when she thanked him. The girl with the goat had sometimes let her stroke the goat's nose while she wrapped up a cheese for her. And even though no one else was quite like Mr. Wainwright, Doxie had expected that at least some of them would show her sympathy, if not real kindness.

Nothing could have been further from the truth. When Doxie had asked the girl with the goat for help, the girl had shouted at her and stood defensively in front of her goat, telling her to go away and not even to think of stealing anything from her stall. Doxie had stumbled off, confused, and gone to ask the baker for a heel of stale bread; as soon as he realized she had no money, the baker spat at her feet and cursed her with names Doxie hadn't even heard before.

It was the same with everyone else in the market square. After every failed attempt to get help, Doxie would sit down on a corner for a little while, hoping not to attract so much attention that she was driven right out of the square. Then she would try again, and time and time again, she was screamed at, berated, told that she was a bad girl who deserved to be thrown out of the orphanage.

Darkness had fallen and all the vendors had gone by the time Doxie crawled, hungry and exhausted, underneath the meager amount of shelter offered by Mr. Wainwright's stall. He had packed up all his boxes of leftover produce and pushed them away on a wheelbarrow. All that remained now was the makeshift table and the shelter he had built over the stall, which was constructed from some bent sticks and a few ragged blankets. They whipped disconsolately in the rising wind as Doxie sat down in the back corner.

She could hardly believe the world was so cold and cruel. Perhaps the other stallholders had noticed something about her, something wrong and awful, as though the crime Mrs. Boggs had accused her of was written loudly across her forehead. Perhaps it really was true that without money, even life had no value.

Tears flowed down her cheeks, blessedly warm only for an instant until the wind turned them ice cold, too. She dropped her head to her knees and wept quietly into her threadbare dress, a small and hungry girl weeping all the tears of a shattered heart. And in the length and breadth of London, no one knew or cared.

CHAPTER 6

THE SOUND of a little child's laughter dragged Doxie's consciousness from a deep sleep. Her eyes felt swollen and scratchy; she kept them closed, listening to the giggles. There was more than one child, she thought; they were laughing at something, enjoying themselves. One of them was Trudy, she knew. She wondered vaguely what it was in that awful orphanage that they could be happy about, but only briefly. She was just glad that there was something bringing them a little joy...

Something prodded her shoulder. Letting out a groan, Doxie turned over, and something uncomfortable scraped across her knee, bringing her a little closer to wakefulness. The giggles turned to voices.

"I told you she ain't dead," said a piping young voice.

"She looked dead," said another – a boy. "She still looks dead to me."

"But she groaned," spoke a third voice; this one was a girl's.

"You can groan when you're dead," said the second voice with great authority.

"How do you know that?" asked the girl.

"Because I poked that old man that died in the gutter in front of the tenement, and he groaned," said the second boy, "but there were maggots in his eyes."

"She doesn't have any maggots," said the first boy. "I'm telling you, she's alive."

"Poke her again," suggested the girl.

Another poke, this time in the back, brought Doxie sharply to wakefulness. She sat up, realising suddenly how very cold she was; her skin was covered with goosebumps, and she was shivering. Wrapping her arms around herself, she blinked into the bright sunlight and felt utter confusion for a long moment. Why was it light in her room? How could she have overslept so much?

Then she saw the barrels, the rags, and realised that she was in old Mr. Wainwright's stall, and that she was alone.

Or at least, she felt alone. In reality, three small children were staring up at her – two boys and a girl. The bigger of the boys held a stick; the girl's eyes were wide and cornflower-blue as she gazed up at Doxie, her mouth slightly open in awe.

"I told you she's not dead," said the big boy confidently.

"Are you dead?" asked the smaller boy.

"No!" Doxie shivered. "I'm alive."

"I told you," repeated the big boy.

"Are you a fairy?" asked the girl.

Despite the hunger throbbing in the pit of her stomach, Doxie felt herself melting at the sight of those wide blue eyes. The little girl seemed awestruck by her, and no matter how cold and hungry and afraid she was, she just had to bring a little spark of wonder to that child's sad and dreary day.

"Yes," she said.

"You're a bit dirty, for a fairy," said the girl.

"I'm – I'm a city fairy," said Doxie, enjoying the fantasy. "I'm not as pretty as my country cousins, but I can do a little magic, too."

"Magic?" The girl stepped forward, her eyes and mouth wide.

"She's lying, Posy," said the big boy. "She's just a tramp."

Just a tramp. The words seared Doxie's soul, and she felt she might have lost herself entirely if she hadn't found her anchor in Posy's eyes. She found a smile somewhere deep within herself, and casting a glance around to make sure that no one else was watching, she reached into her pocket.

"Ready to see some magic?" she asked.

Posy's eyes brightened. "Yes," she whispered.

Doxie pulled the spoon out of her pocket and spun it in the sunlight, then dropped it back safely into her apron. It was a trick she had done a few times for the smaller children, when no one was watching; she moved too quickly for anyone to see what the flash of silver really was. But it always dazzled them, and it dazzled Posy now. She let out a cry of delight and stretched her arms toward Doxie, then clasped them to her mouth.

"A fairy! A fairy!" she cried. "You really are a fairy!"

"Emmett! Posy! Jonathan!" barked a feminine voice. "Get away from there!"

The two boys began to shuffle away, but Posy rushed to Doxie and seized the sleeve of her dress. "Come with me. Come!" she said, tugging insistently. "I have to show you to my mama!"

Doxie tugged back, terrified. "No – no!" she gasped.

It was too late. Posy had yanked Doxie up to the front of the stall, and there she stood – the thin, bedraggled woman who had been making gruel yesterday, the one Doxie had avoided. Fear struck deep into the pit of Doxie's stomach at the sight of her now. Her features were so pinched, and her eyes were deeply hooded. There was something cold and bitter about the set of her mouth, and an ugly, hairy mole stuck out on her left cheekbone.

"What are you talking about, Posy?" she barked.

"She's a fairy, Mama," said Posy. "She's a city fairy."

"I…" Doxie began.

"Come away from her." The thin woman seized Posy's arm and yanked her closer. "What are you doing with my daughter?"

"Nothing, m-ma'am," Doxie stammered. "I – I was just sleeping."

"We thought she was dead," said the bigger of the two boys. "Then we poked her with a stick, and she wasn't."

"She wasn't hurting us, Mama," said Posy quietly. "She wouldn't. Fairies are good and kind."

The woman sighed, her eyes traveling over Doxie's thin and tattered body. She looked down at Posy, who grinned at her. "Isn't she a pretty fairy?" the child asked.

To Doxie's surprise, a smile tugged at the corners of the thin woman's mouth. "Yes, darling," she said, her voice filling with unexpected warmth. She trailed her fingertips around the round edge of Posy's cheek. "Almost as pretty as you are. Why, I haven't seen you smile in such a long time." The woman looked up, her eyes locking on Doxie. "And it's this girl who made you smile so."

Doxie was trembling. She backed away a little. "I don't want any trouble, ma'am," she said nervously.

"How old are you, child?" the woman asked.

Doxie swallowed hard. "About nine," she said.

"Poor thing. Where are your parents?"

Doxie dropped her eyes to the floor. "I don't have any."

"And why aren't you in the orphanage?"

There it was. Doxie's stomach clenched.

"I – I was thrown out," she said, a lump growing in her throat. "I was thrown out, but I didn't mean to do anything wrong. I was just trying to help the little baby. I didn't want to make anyone angry. I only wanted to help." Tears started streaming down her cheeks, sobs tearing at her chest. "Oh, please, ma'am, I didn't want to hurt Posy either. I just wanted to make her smile a little."

The woman came closer. Doxie cowered, but the hand that rested on her shoulder was gentle.

"And you did, little one," said the woman. "You made my Posy smile – something no one has been able to do in a very long time." The hand squeezed gently. "What's your name?"

Doxie raised her face. The woman's eyes held an improbable warmth.

"Doxie," she whispered.

"Well, Doxie, how would you like something to eat and somewhere warm to sleep in exchange for staying at my tenement and caring for my two smallest girls?" asked the woman. "They're sickly little things, and I can't be there with them. I'd be grateful if you could."

Doxie swallowed her tears, her heart leaping within her. Perhaps she was still worth something after all, worthy of the silver spoon in her pocket and whatever it signified.

"Oh, please, ma'am," she whispered. "Please. I would love that."

"Good. Then come with me." The woman took her hand, gripping it gently the way no adult had ever held her hand before. "My name is Mabel Lee, and you're going to be just fine."

She led Doxie out of the marketplace, with Doxie's heart fluttering with hope. Even though Doxie missed Trudy and Owen and the others with everything inside her, perhaps Mabel was right. Perhaps things were going to work out after all.

Doxie had thought that the orphanage was drafty and cold, but it was nothing compared to the tenement where Mabel and the children lived.

When she saw the narrow, four-story building leaning precariously upon its neighbors, looking like it had been shoved into the gap between two stronger buildings as an afterthought, Doxie thought that perhaps the Lees lived on one of the floors. The building was so thin that each floor could hardly contain two of the rooms back in the orphanage.

Instead, when they climbed the stairs to the top floor, Doxie found out that not one family was living on it, but four.

The floor had been partitioned off roughly into four rooms with bits of scrap wood, sheets of rusty metal and even threadbare sheets used as inadequate curtains. Doxie felt instantly as though she would suffocate from the pressure of overcrowded humanity around her. The smell was unspeakable; the very air was thick with smoke and dust. There was a reek of unwashed bodies, an undertone of dusky mold, and through the many drafts around the one-brick-thin walls and the boarded-up window, a rising stench came in from the street.

Mabel did not appear to be affected by the squalor. Carrying Posy on her hip, she led Doxie across the room to the section at the back, on the left. Pushing aside a tattered sheet, she led her into the tiny space that her family called home. There were five children and Mabel, yet the room was less than half of the size of Doxie's dormitory back in the orphanage. There were no beds. In one corner, a pallet lay on the floor, a few crumpled blankets lying upon it. There was a bucket in the other. Nearest the entrance, on Doxie's left, there was an old coal-scuttle, soot-blackened and warped as though Mabel had been building a fire right there inside it.

"Mama's home, girls," Mabel called in an unexpectedly soft voice.

The heap of blankets on the pallet twitched and was pushed aside, and the two thinnest, palest toddlers that Doxie had ever seen – which was saying something – looked up from where they had been lying. They were emaciated children, their eyes huge in their pinched faces, their little dresses hanging shapelessly from bony frames. A constant stream of mucus ran from the nose of one; the other had unnaturally red cheeks, as though she were feverish. Mabel set Posy down on the ground and went over to them, wiping a nose here, feeling a forehead there.

"Are you hungry, my babies?" she asked softly.

"Yes, Mama," piped up the runny-nosed one. Her curls were so dirty that it was hard to tell what colour they'd once been, but Doxie's guess was blonde.

"And you, little Daffy?" asked Mabel quietly.

The rosy-cheeked one shook her head. Mabel felt her forehead again, then looked up at Doxie over her shoulder. Her eyes shone with a quiet desperation.

"They're never well," she said softly. "They were sickly babies, too. Twins." She shook her head, her eyes growing haunted. "Their birth was difficult. But it was last winter that really took it out of them." She sighed, brushing the blonde one's curls out of her eyes. "I can't take them out into the cold anymore. But I can't bear to leave them here all alone."

Doxie walked over to Mabel, stretching out her arms to Daffy. The child gripped them automatically, allowing herself to be lifted and cradled.

"Hello," she said, smiling down at her. "My name's Doxie."

A smile flickered around the corners of the child's lips. She wiped at her nose with the back of a hand.

"Doxie's a fairy, Daffy," said Posy brightly. "She's come to look after you with her magic."

Daffy's eyes widened. "Magic?" she whispered.

The word made Doxie's heart falter within her. Here in this place, this place that was even worse than the orphanage, Doxie felt that there was no magic in the world at all. Perhaps it had all died somehow, or perhaps it had been left in the orphanage.

She didn't know what to say to Daffy. She just smiled at her instead, her heart pounding uncomfortably behind her breastbone.

"Just stay with them, Doxie," said Mabel, setting the other twin down on the pallet. "You've met Daffy – this is Tulip." Her smile faltered. "I like flower names." She sighed. "Keep them warm if you can, and there's a little tea. Give them that if they're hungry. I'll be home with supper as soon as I can."

"Can I stay here with Doxie, Mama?" Posy asked.

"No." Mabel straightened, her jaw clenching. "You have to go begging with your brothers, Posy, you know that. Come on. Let's go."

With that, the three of them were gone, and Doxie was left alone in the reeking tenement surrounded by strangers. She sat down on the pallet, pulling the unresisting bodies of the two tiny girls into her lap, and held them as close as she could.

PART II

CHAPTER 7

Six Months Later

THERE WAS no room on the sleeping pallet for everyone. Mabel slept there, her arms wrapped around Emmett and Jonathan, Posy curled up against her back. Daffy and Tulip lay by her feet, cuddled up close to their mother's legs as the last coals of the fire in the scuttle produced little other than the smoke that hung low in the cramped room, making eyes water and noses run.

Doxie could hear little Tulip sniffling from where she lay curled on the pile of old newspapers that served as her own bed. Head pillowed on her arm, she listened to the child's labored breathing. It turned to coughing, a wet, sucking sound that scared Doxie, followed by a silence that made her heart ache. Then the harsh, labored panting started again.

Newspapers crackled under Doxie as she stirred. Immediately, she regretted it. She had just started to warm up the hollow in the newspapers where she was lying, and the moment she moved, the thin blanket that Mabel had given her lifted up at one corner, allowing an icy draft to blow right down Doxie's back.

In the distance, the bell of some far-flung church chimed, barely audible over the heavy breathing of the many sleepers in this ugly tenement. It was just after ten, but Mabel and the other children were fast asleep, exhausted from a long day out on the streets.

Tulip coughed again. Doxie sat up, the blanket falling around her knees and exposing her shoulders to the savage wind.

"Tulip?" she whispered.

In the dim light filtering through the tatty curtain, the blankets on the sleeping pallet stirred, then fell back. A tousled head of blonde curls emerged, still coughing.

"I'm cold," Tulip choked out between the coughs.

Mabel stirred, mumbling in her sleep. Doxie didn't want her rest to be disturbed. She held out her arms. "Come here, love," she said. "I'll tuck you in."

Tulip didn't need telling twice. She slipped out from under the blanket, dropping it back down over her siblings, and padded across the grubby floor. Doxie wrapped the little child in her arms, feeling the hard, bony edges of her angular body as she tucked the blanket around Tulip. It didn't quite fit over both of them; a little of Doxie's back couldn't be covered, and the draft chilled her right through the thinning fabric of her dress. Still, Tulip's body in her arms was wonderfully warm. The child coughed again, tucking her head under Doxie's chin.

Perhaps she was too warm. Doxie pressed her cheek to Tulip's forehead. "Don't you feel well, darling?" she whispered.

Tulip shook her head a little. Doxie bit her lip, her body tightening with fear. Tulip had been sickly when Doxie first came to live with the Lees, but she had improved with Doxie constantly keeping her warm and hydrated. In fact, summer had been beautiful; there had been a few days when Doxie could take Tulip and Daffy down to the little park on the far end of the slum, and the girls could play like normal children for a few minutes, even though the walk almost exhausted them.

But this winter had been brutal. Just a few weeks ago, Tulip had been sick like this, and Doxie had feared for the little girl's life. It seemed she had rallied just in time, yet Doxie didn't like the sound of her cough now.

"My chest is sore," Tulip mumbled, her words babyish and garbled.

Doxie stroked the wayward curls. "Don't worry, darling," she whispered. "Just sleep for now. We'll get you some medicine in the morning." She knew it was a lie. Mabel was barely able to feed them all, let alone buy medicine.

She held Tulip a little tighter as the child's labored breathing grew slower, more rhythmic. Even as she drifted off to sleep, there was still a terrible rattle in her lungs with every breath.

"Doxie?"

Doxie lifted her head. Daffy was standing in front of her, twisting the skirt of her too-big dress in both of her small hands.

"Yes, love?" Doxie whispered.

"Can I lie with you?" Daffy asked. "Emmett keeps pulling the blanket off me."

"Of course, darling." Doxie shifted a little on the newspapers. "Come here."

Daffy crawled in behind Doxie, wrapping her thin arms around Doxie's body, a little hand resting on Doxie's side. It was gloriously warm, and the warmth seemed to spread right into the cold and weary corners of Doxie's tired heart.

"COME ON, TULIP." Doxie forced a smile as she clutched the bowl of yesterday's cold gruel. It had congealed in the bottom of the cracked wooden bowl; Doxie had to hold it tightly to keep it from pulling apart and spilling the precious food onto the floor. She dug a small wooden spoon into the mushy substance and held it out. "One more bite."

Tulip shook her head. She was leaning against the back wall, sitting on the sleeping pallet with the blankets tangled around her legs. She refused to let Doxie tuck them around her despite the chilly air; her skin was burning to the touch.

"You need your strength, darling," said Doxie. "Come on. One bite."

"I'll eat it," said Daffy. She was sitting at Doxie's feet, and she scooted a little closer, her wide, innocent eyes fixed on Doxie. "I will."

"Maybe in a minute, Daffy." Doxie forced a smile. "Let's see if Tulip wants her share first."

"I – don't," Tulip moaned, her words coming out on racing breaths. "I just – want – to sleep."

There was a yelp from behind Doxie. She glanced over her shoulder to see Jonathan and Emmett sitting next to each other, sharing a bowl of gruel. Emmett was giving his younger brother a murderous look, and Doxie guessed that they weren't sharing well.

"Boys!" Mabel snapped. "You know the rules. Half for each of you. No cheating."

She was standing by the door, checking through the cast iron pot to make sure the few bits of equipment she owned were still inside it: a matchbox, a wooden spoon, half a sack of oats. The matchbox rattled ominously when she shook it, and she sighed, her shoulders slumping.

Doxie turned back to Tulip. "Please, sweetheart," she coaxed. "One more."

"No!" Tulip coughed the word forcefully, throwing herself down on the pallet and tugging at the blankets. "No more!"

"All right. All right." Doxie pulled the blankets around her, grateful that the child was allowing it. "Here, Daffy." She placed the bowl in Daffy's small hands.

The little girl gave a gasp of delight and began wolfing down the gruel. It was gone in three bites, and she busied herself with licking the bowl, trying to get every morsel of food out of it.

"Time to go, children," said Mabel firmly. She got up, lifting the pot. "Hurry up now."

Emmett pushed Jonathan to the ground, and Jonathan squealed.

"Stop that!" Mabel snapped. "Let's go."

"Come on, boys." Doxie grabbed an arm apiece and lifted the boys to their feet. "It's a nice day outside. Perhaps you can play in the snow a little when you're done with begging."

"All right, Doxie," said Emmett meekly. He smiled at her.

"There, that's better." Doxie ruffled his hair. "Now, go on."

The boys hurried down the makeshift hall, closely pursued by little Posy. Doxie smiled after them, turning to go back to the sleeping pallet. Mabel reached out a hand. "Doxie, wait."

Doxie looked up at her, a little surprised. Mabel already had her pot hanging from her hand; she seldom spoke to Doxie, or anyone, this early in the morning. She was saving her strength for the market, Doxie knew.

"Yes, ma'am?" Doxie said, a little nervous.

Mabel glanced out of the room. Emmett, Jonathan and Posy were gone; they must already be halfway down the stairs. She shot a glance at the two little girls, then let out a sigh and fixed Doxie with a steady look from those surprisingly clear, calm eyes.

"Tulip is dying," she said.

Doxie reeled back, shocked at the frankness of Mabel's tone.

"She's all right, ma'am," she cried. "She's just..." Her voice trailed off in the face of Mabel's serious eyes. She thought of the rattling of Tulip's breath, of the way she refused food and water, and she knew Mabel was right.

"There's no use in denying it, Doxie," said Mabel softly. "We have to find a way to help her..." Her voice trailed off. "I'm going to do my best in the market today. But if there's anything, anything you can do... I need you to do it."

Doxie thought instantly of the silver spoon resting in the pocket of her apron, but everything inside her recoiled at the thought. That spoon was all she had. She couldn't give it up, not if she could find another way to look after Tulip.

"I'll find something, Mabel," she said. "I'll go out today if the weather is nice enough, and take them with me, and I'll find money. I'll beg if I have to. I'll do whatever I need to do."

Mabel rested a hand on Doxie's shoulder, a sad smile lifting the corners of her mouth.

"Posy was right, you know," she said. "You might not be a fairy, but there's a little magic in you. Do your best, child."

The kind words were as unexpected as a bright ray of sunshine piercing storm clouds, and Doxie stood stunned for a few seconds even after Mabel had left the room. Then she squared her shoulders, turning back to where the two little girls lay.

She wasn't going to let them or their mother down. No matter what it took, she had to find a way to save Tulip.

DAFFY CLUNG to Doxie's skirt with both hands, tugging at the aged fabric. It pulled uncomfortably around her waist and thighs with every step she took, and she could feel the seams loosen with the force of the toddler's pulling.

Walking was hard enough with Tulip on her hip. Tulip's arms were draped loosely around Doxie's neck, her head cradled on Doxie's shoulder, but she hung in her arms like a dead weight. *No.* Doxie didn't want to think about the word *dead,* even though the sound of Tulip's breathing terrified her now more than ever.

"It's going to be all right, pet," she murmured, tucking the blanket between Tulip's shoulder and her own. It was the only protection she could bring with her against the cold spring breeze that blew thinly down the grey street.

"Legs tired," mumbled Daffy's small voice. She slowed down even more, creating a harder tug on Doxie's skirt. This time, Doxie was sure she heard a seam rip.

"Daffy!" She stopped, looking down at the little girl, and the annoyance that had flared in her heart died at once at the sight of the tears that had washed twin trails down Daffy's grubby cheeks. How long had she been crying quietly as she clung to Doxie's dress?

They had been walking for a long time. Doxie wasn't sure just how long, but it was past noon; the sun was slipping down the western sky. She had tried begging on every street corner she knew, but Tulip's cough was driving people away, and frustration was rising constantly in Doxie's heart. Yet poor Daffy looked as though she was weeping from sheer exhaustion.

"Legs tired," Daffy repeated quietly.

"I know, poppet, but it's not too much further," said Doxie.

"Where we going?" asked Daffy.

In truth, Doxie didn't know. The next street corner, or the next marketplace, might yield some kind stranger who would bother to throw a few pennies in the direction of three ragged children.

"It's not much further," she repeated helplessly.

Daffy let out a great sigh. "Legs tired," she said again, her knees buckling.

"Daffy, no!" Doxie cried, but it was too late. The little girl had already flopped down to the ground, sitting cross-legged on the cold and filthy pavement.

Tulip gave another horrible, retching cough on Doxie's shoulder. Her chest sounded like a box of stones. Doxie felt urgency rising within her. "Get up, Daffy," she said.

Daffy stretched up her thin arms. "Carry me," she said.

"I can't," said Doxie. "I'm carrying Tulip."

"Tulip walk." Daffy's face grew grim with determination. "Carry me!"

Doxie wanted to scream. How could she explain to this toddler that her sister couldn't walk because she was... sick? *Dying*. The word Mabel had used came back to her, running down the length of her spine like a rodent, and she shook it off with a shudder of her whole body.

"Daffy, you need to get up," she said.

"Carry!" Daffy howled.

Doxie looked around the street in desperation, as if something could inspire her about this run-down street with its tiny houses and miserable tenements. Improbably enough, something did. Her eye rested on a young woman hurrying down the street, a bundle of rags clutched tightly in her arms. The bundle cried thinly; it had to be an infant, even though it was wrapped in the kind of rags that a rich woman would shudder to use on her floors. The woman, too, wore threadbare clothing, but there was something in her hand that flashed like a jewel.

It was a medicine bottle, deep red and cut from fine glass, and Doxie's heart thumped. She would give anything to find something similar for Tulip.

"Excuse me!" Ignoring Daffy, Doxie stepped into the young woman's path. "Hello – excuse me!"

The woman stopped. She had the wary eyes of a wild thing, the quick movements of one of the feral cats that used to squabble and steal from the dustbins outside the orphanage.

"I don't mean any trouble." Doxie took a step nearer, holding Tulip a little tighter as the child let out another of those terrible, painful coughs. "I just want to know where you got that... that medicine."

The woman's grip tightened on the bottle. "You can't have it," she said, her voice frightened as she glanced around, trying to find a way to pass Doxie without coming too close. "My baby needs it. The doctor says he'll die without it."

"I'd never take it from you," said Doxie. "Please, I just want to know – which doctor saw you? Was it expensive?"

The woman's eyes traveled to Tulip, then to Daffy, then back to Doxie, and finally relented a little. She relaxed just enough to stop squeezing her baby quite so tightly, and began to bounce it gently instead, soothing its cries.

"Just down the street, there's an old Catholic church," she said. "The doctor runs a clinic there every Wednesday. He'll still be there. He'll help you, if you're quick. And it don't cost anything."

"Nothing?" Doxie's heart thudded.

"Nothing. But it's busy. You might be too late," said the woman. Her eyes went to Tulip again. "Good luck," she said softly, and then, pushing past Doxie, she was gone.

Doxie turned around. "Daffy, get up," she said, crouching awkwardly – her back aching with the strain of holding Tulip

– to grab the little girl's hand. "We're nearly there. Right down the street."

Daffy dragged herself to her feet. "What's a doctor?" she asked.

"It's a nice man who's going to help us," said Doxie.

She could only pray that that was true.

CHAPTER 8

THE LINE GOING into the square, squat building of the clinic seemed impossibly long. Doxie waited behind a fat man with a terrible wheeze, his skin holding a bluish tinge. Daffy was crying loudly with exhaustion; she stroked the little girl's hair, trying to soothe her as she bounced Tulip on her hip. Tulip seemed too listless to cry or even to cough. The silence frightened her.

The sun continued to slip down the western sky. Doxie had done her best not to stray too far from the tenement, but she knew that it was still at least a half an hour's walk home, and she grew more and more frightened that she might have to walk home in the dark. She switched Tulip from arm to arm, but eventually both of them were equally numb, so she just cradled the little sick girl in her arms. Every few minutes, the line would grow a little shorter, and Doxie would cling a little tighter to what hope she had left.

Finally, somehow, Doxie found herself standing in front of a door with paint so faded and peeling that there was more bare wood to be seen than painted surface. Tulip was breathing raggedly; Doxie bounced her gently, trying to keep her calm. Daffy had grown too exhausted to cry. She simply sat on the ground at Doxie's feet in a motionless little heap, her head pillowed on her knees, dozing off into brief fits of slumber.

Doxie felt as though both her arms were in danger of dropping off when the door opened at last. An elderly man limped out, holding a jar of ointment. Behind him, a tired-looking man in his middle age blinked out at Doxie from behind thick round spectacles. He had a neatly trimmed beard and was going very bald on the top of his head; his coat looked as though it had been well-cut once, but its white had faded to grey.

The eyes were so tired and sad that Doxie almost wanted to apologize for adding to this man's burdens. But the sound of Tulip's breathing was making her desperate. Clutching the child a little closer, she croaked out the only words that would come to her mind. "Please, sir."

The doctor's eyes skimmed over Tulip's little body. "Come," he said, stepping back.

With Daffy trailing along behind, Doxie carried Tulip into a tiny room with flaking paint and a long crack in one wall.

There was a trunk against one wall, a black bag balancing atop it; against the other wall, a narrow bunk. A basin set in the back wall had only one tap.

"Set her down here," said the doctor, indicating the bed.

Doxie lowered Tulip to the bed as gently as she could. It was a blessed relief to finally put down that weight; bony though she was, Tulip had grown very heavy as the hours ticked past. The little girl's eyes opened when Doxie let her go, and she stared up at the doctor for a long second but seemed too exhausted to be afraid. Lying there limply, she submitted to the doctor's examination. Doxie stood against the opposite wall, trembling with fear and exhaustion and holding little Daffy's hand firmly in her own.

It seemed to take very long for the doctor to listen to Tulip's lungs, place a thermometer in her mouth and feel over her thin limbs. Finally, he turned to Doxie, and his eyes held a sorrowful resignation more frightening than any amount of worry.

"Is she your sister, child?" he asked. His voice was unexpectedly tender.

"No, sir," said Doxie. "I just take care of her." She felt a lump growing in her throat at the sight of Tulip's tiny body lying there on that bed. "I do my best, sir," she cried, and burst into tears.

They were tears of terror and exhaustion, and the doctor crouched down beside her, resting his big hands on her shoulders. "There, there, child," he said, his voice calm and stern. "I know it's hard, but you mustn't give in. These children need you."

The words made Doxie's tears dry up. Gulping at the lump in her throat, she squared her shoulders and looked up into the doctor's eyes. "Please, sir," she said. "What's wrong with Tulip?"

"Well, I don't think it's consumption," said the doctor gently. "That's good news. But she has a fever and an infection of her lungs." He paused. "I will give you some medicine, which will keep her comfortable for a little while, but there's one thing she needs far more than medicine."

Doxie swallowed hard. "What is it, doctor?" she asked.

The doctor's eyes softened. "Food," he said. "The whole reason why this child is so ill is because she's malnourished." He gestured at Daffy. "This one, too – and probably you, as well. You all need to be properly nourished."

Doxie felt as though the last of her strength was leaving her. She barely stopped herself from sinking to the floor in dismay. "We don't have food," she breathed. "We don't have money, or anything."

"I know." The doctor shook his head. "But that doesn't change the truth." He paused. "Perhaps you might think of going into a workhouse."

Doxie had thought of that too, but Mabel fiercely resisted any mention of a workhouse. She had told Doxie that that would mean separation from all of her children, and the boys being taken away from the girls. It was too much for Doxie to think about, let alone for Mabel to bear.

"They'll be taken from their mama." Doxie's eyes filled with tears. "I'll find another way."

"There may not be another way," said the doctor gently.

"There has to be!" Doxie's voice came out with more force than she had intended. "I'll find a way. I'll find another way." She was suddenly overwhelmed with fear that Tulip would be taken away from her, and she hurried to the child, pulling her into her arms and backing toward the door. "I'll find a way," she said again.

"All right – don't go." The doctor rummaged in his bag and pulled out a greenish bottle. "Give her a little of this now, and again after supper. It'll help to make her more comfortable."

Doxie took it from his hand. Their eyes met, and the doctor's were filled with sorrow. "Godspeed to you, child," he said. "I hope the little one gets better."

Doxie hurried out of the door, the doctor's last words sending a chill down her spine. She wished he had told her that Tulip *would* get better, and quickly. Instead, all he had to offer her was his hope.

It didn't feel like enough. Doxie stared down at the child's flushed cheeks, her sweaty hair clinging to her emaciated face, and determination rose in her. She was going to find a way to save Tulip – just as soon as she'd taken her home and given her that medicine.

"Hold on, little one," Doxie whispered, pressing her lips close against the child's cheek. "Just hold on."

BY THE TIME Doxie walked into the tenement, the three other children had already come home from begging. As soon as she pushed through the curtain, Posy's little voice cried out, "There they are!"

The little girl came running across the floor toward Doxie and her two younger sisters. She threw her arms around Doxie's knees. "You're back," she said.

"We didn't know where you were." Emmett folded his arms, giving Doxie a baleful glare born of worry. "We didn't know if Tulip and Daffy were all right."

"I'm fine. We're all fine," said Doxie.

No, we're not, she thought to herself. *Tulip is dying, and I have to find food for her – now*. She bit her lip. "How did begging go today?" she asked.

"It was all right. We got a few pennies. We gave them to Mama at the market, and she told us to come home," said Emmett.

Doxie had hoped that perhaps Mabel had already given the children some food to bring home. She stumbled over to the sleeping pallet and lowered Tulip's hot little form onto the blankets. Daffy had already collapsed in the corner, her face pale, exhausted beyond expression. Doxie fished in her apron pocket for the medicine bottle; it clanged musically against her spoon.

"Where were you?" asked Emmett.

"What's that?" asked Jonathan.

"I took Tulip to the doctor," said Doxie. "This is medicine for her."

"Is it magic?" asked Posy.

"I hope so, darling," said Doxie. "Come on, Tulip. You have to drink this."

The little girl shook her head, screwing her small fists into her eyes. Doxie gritted her teeth, dismay assailing her. What if she couldn't get Tulip to drink it? "Come on, love," she said. "Please. It'll help you. You'll feel better."

"Don't want," wailed Tulip.

"Tulip, it's fairy magic," said Posy. "It's going to make you all better."

Tulip lowered her hands, her wide eyes fixing on the bottle. With the grubby sunlight striking it from behind, it sparkled a little, and the child was convinced. Doxie was able to pour a small trickle of the medicine down her throat; she swallowed, and Doxie stoppered the bottle, then placed it carefully in the box that contained the Lees' only possessions.

"Now you all stay here," she said. "Emmett, Jonathan, take care of your sisters." Emmett was the eldest at seven, but it would have to do.

"Where are you going?" demanded Emmett.

Doxie paused at the curtain, turning back to give them a smile she couldn't feel. "I'm just going to find something to eat," she said. "I'll be right back."

"But it's time for my nap." Posy came closer, clutching Doxie's skirt in her little hands. "You have to sing to me."

Doxie knew she needed to say no and go outside and find food to keep Tulip and Daffy alive, but she couldn't say no to those blue eyes. She took a deep breath and reached for Posy's hand. "One song, all right?" she said. "That's all for today."

"Just one," agreed Posy solemnly. "The magic fairy song."

Doxie wasn't sure how the few bars of "Home, Sweet Home" she knew had become known to Posy as "the magic fairy song", but she wasn't about to complain. That song and the spoon had been the two things that had stayed with Doxie since she'd been thrown out of the orphanage.

She settled Posy on the sleeping pallet between her two sisters – feeling the fever warmth of little Tulip's body – and covered them all with a musty blanket. She stroked Posy's hair as she sang, the familiar bars of the old song filling the tiny room, but softly; the other people on this floor didn't appreciate her singing.

She sang both stanzas before Posy's eyes finally closed. Here, in this cold tenement, with the starving children, with the rattling of Tulip's labored breaths, the fantasy of home felt a long, long way away. Doxie wondered if she would ever truly know it. If she would ever feel safe and warm somewhere.

A place where we're warm and the fire burns bright;

a place where we're safe and cosy at night.

Home! Home! Sweet home!

CHAPTER 9

DOXIE'S HEART felt cold and grim within her as she walked out into the gathering darkness. She avoided the market where Mabel was selling gruel; she knew Mabel would never agree with the plan she had made in order to get the girls some food. But Doxie felt that she had no choice. She had nothing to sell and no one would hire her at this hour, and Tulip and Daffy couldn't wait any longer.

She would have to steal.

It was a brisk half-hour's walk from the tenements to the nicer, more upper-class market square on the very edge of the slum. Here, instead of tattered stalls with starving proprietors as haggard and hungry as the people who bought their rotting and rejected wares, there were real brick-and-mortar shops with lights in the windows and shopkeepers with wide smiles and rosy cheeks. They were all about to close up for the day, Doxie saw. Many of them were sweeping out their shops, counting their money, or even starting to remove the boxes of produce and baked goods from the windows.

It was the bakery window that looked the most appealing to her, mostly because she could carry plenty of bread in her thin arms, even if it got a little crushed along the way. The baker was a bent little old man with a shock of white hair and a bald patch in the middle of his crown; he didn't seem as though he'd be able to put up a fight if he caught her.

Doxie's stomach clenched. He looked like such a sweet little old man, chatting with his portly wife who was behind the counter, sweeping out his shop in stiff little movements. She knew that stealing from him would be appalling and wrong. But letting Tulip die would be a thousand, no, an infinite number of times worse. She had to do this.

Taking a deep breath, Doxie crept out of her hiding place between two of the shops and darted across the street, ducking among the rattling evening traffic. There was a muffled curse from a young man on the sidewalk as she brushed past him, and her heart thudded hard. She didn't want to call attention to herself. She just needed to grab some bread from that window.

Pausing in the shadows at the corner of the bakery, Doxie waited for her heart to slow down just a little. There was a wicker tray of bread within arm's reach of the door. If she was quick, she could run up to the door, grab the entire tray, and bolt. It would be more than enough to keep Tulip and Daffy's bellies full for a whole day, and give the other children some extra, besides.

Her heart hammered in her chest. She had to do this. Reaching into her apron pocket, she touched the silver spoon for a moment, and felt strength go into her. It was just enough to make her dart forward. Rushing along the sidewalk, she lunged through the doorway, ducking past the old baker. She heard a cry of alarm; her hands closed on the basket, and she spun to bolt away.

"Thief!" shrieked the old man, swiping at her with his broom. "Stop, thief!"

Doxie ducked the broom, clinging to the tray, and bolted. If she could just get down the street, she could disappear into the city –

A huge hand descended on the back of her dress, grabbing a fistful of cloth. Her dress sprang tightly around her chest; her feet shot out from under her, and though she clung to the tray, the bread flew into the air. As she landed heavily on the ground, a pang of pain running through her body, the breads bounced and rolled away on the dirty paving.

"No!" Doxie choked out.

The hand seized her hair this time. She was wrenched to her feet, pain blossoming through her scalp. Looking up through a mess of hair and stinging soreness, Doxie stared into the granite-hard face of a police officer, all nose and chin looming out from under the black shadow of his polished helmet.

"Thought you were quick enough, did you, you little waif?" snarled the man.

Doxie felt as though her insides had been turned into water. She trembled uncontrollably, terror filling her body. She knew that fighting would be useless. The policeman held a gleaming truncheon in his free hand.

With some huffing and puffing, the baker arrived beside the policeman, stiff-legged, hair in hopeless disarray.

"My bread!" he cried in dismay, looking around at the bread that was lying everywhere; most of the loaves had broken or squashed, and a few were lying in the filthy gutter. "Oh, my bread!"

"I'm sorry about that, sir," said the policeman. "But I've caught the urchin."

The baker looked up from the bread, and his eyes rested on Doxie's face for the first time. Surprise filled his eyes. He took a step nearer, staring at her.

"Why, officer," he said, "she's only a child."

"A criminal nonetheless." The policeman gave Doxie a shake that rattled her teeth and sent pain jolting through her scalp. "Rest assured, sir, she'll be brought to justice."

"Justice?" The baker turned pale. "What do you mean? Will she be sentenced – imprisoned, at her age?"

The policeman shrugged. "She must be punished, sir."

"But she's only a child," said the baker. "Why, she can't be more than eleven years old."

Doxie sensed kindness radiating from the baker, and it made her feel even worse for stealing from him. But far more pressing was her worry over Daffy and Tulip. She had to get back to them. She had to get food to them somehow.

And she could do none of that if she was in prison.

Her heart filled with pain and shock at the realisation of exactly how much trouble she was in. Would she ever see the children again?

"Oh, please, sir!" she cried, panic filling her eyes with tears. "Please, please, I just needed food. Please let me go! I needed food!"

"Stop your fuss!" snapped the policeman, shaking her again.

"Sir, please, I implore you." The baker turned to the policeman. "Can't you see she's only a hungry child? I can bake more bread, but this child cannot starve. Please don't take her to the prison."

Where the policeman had been completely heartless to Doxie's pleas, he softened a little for the baker's. "Well, sir, she's no more than a common thief in my eyes," he said. "But if it pleases you, because you're a good-hearted gentleman, I'll take her to the workhouse instead of the prison."

"No!" Doxie shrieked, terror thrilling through her. The workhouse would take her away from the children, and they were all that she really cared about.

"Don't be frightened, child," said the baker. "You'll be safe there. You'll have food and clothing and an education."

"No! Let me go! Let me go, please!" Doxie sobbed.

"Stop that!" the policeman roared, shaking Doxie so hard that black stars popped in her vision. "You ungrateful little wench!"

"She's only afraid. Please, officer, take her to the workhouse," said the baker.

"As you wish, sir." The policeman gave Doxie's hair a last tug. "Now I'm going to take your arm, child, and you're going to walk beside me, or so help me, I'll teach you a lesson! Do you understand?"

Doxie looked up at the policeman's stony face, his harsh eyes, and she knew that there was no escaping her fate. Tears poured down her cheeks. She had failed Daffy and Tulip, and Emmett and Jonathan, and poor, sweet Posy. She had failed all of them, just as she had failed the orphanage.

Sobbing, she allowed the policeman to lock his gigantic fist around her little arm and drag her down the street.

THE MATRON of the workhouse had the longest face that Doxie had ever seen, with a thin, bitter mouth that looked like it had been pencilled on, one grey arc with both points facing down. It was as though those down-turned corners of the mouth had dragged the matron's entire face with it, her jowls sagging down from lean temples, her nose making an angry hook. Her eyes looked the colour and temperature of frozen mud.

She had received Doxie from the policeman with hardly a word. The policeman had frightened Doxie right out of her tears in the brisk walk from the bakery to the workhouse, and now Doxie's arm ached from being wrenched every time she made a sound or displeased him. She hugged it tightly to her chest, her heart beating wildly as she followed the matron down a cold grey hallway.

There were bars on all the windows. So far, Doxie couldn't see the difference between this workhouse and prison.

The matron pushed open a door to her right. "Come in here," she ordered.

They were the first words she'd spoken directly to Doxie. Trembling with horror, Doxie obeyed. Was the matron taking her to a cell?

Instead, the room looked like the biggest, coldest bathroom Doxie had ever seen. There was a big tub in the corner with two taps; the water inside looked as though someone had already used it – it was cloudy grey and there was no steam rising from it. The door slammed behind Doxie, and she spun around to face the matron, who looked both bitter and bored.

"Take off your clothing and bathe yourself," she ordered. "Wash your hair, too."

Doxie's heart thumped. She knew exactly what would happen if this matron discovered the silver spoon lying in her pocket, and she couldn't bear the thought.

"P-pardon me?" she stammered, trying to buy herself a little time.

"You heard me, child," snapped the matron. She went over to the rack in the corner, where ugly, striped dresses were hanging in a long row, all different sizes, all of them well-worn. "Get undressed."

The matron started rifling through the dresses, and Doxie quickly yanked the spoon from her pocket, hiding it in her hand. She struggled to pull off her dress with the spoon clenched tightly in her fingers. It felt wrong and frightening to be naked in this cold room with this strange woman, but

Doxie was far more worried about the spoon as she tiptoed over to the horrifying bath.

"Get in, child," the matron ordered as Doxie clutched the spoon in front of her. "The water's already half cold as it is."

The water was more than half cold. Doxie gasped as it lapped around her body, instantly raising goosebumps on her skin, but the cold water was the least of her worries. The spoon was still in her hand, but the matron had taken a dress off the rack; she knew that at any moment the bitter old woman would turn around and see the spoon in her hand...

Doxie's desperate eyes were casting around for a solution when she spotted it. The walls were brick, their mortar crumbling, and there was a niche between two of the bricks, just big enough and dark enough to hide a silver spoon. Quick as she could, Doxie wedged the spoon into the gap. It fit perfectly, sliding neatly out of sight.

Miss Claire's words came back to her. *A little miracle, if you will.* Doxie's heart flipped over at the thought.

"Come on, child," snapped the matron. "Head too, for the lice."

Taking a deep breath, Doxie plunged into the icy water. Unwelcome hands reached into the bath and scrubbed her, holding her down for a moment longer than was comfortable to roughly scrub her matted hair. She came up gasping, and the matron was ready with a towel.

Doxie allowed herself to be bundled in the towel and scrubbed dry. She allowed herself to have the ugly, striped dress pulled over her head, where it clung to her still-damp and shivering body. And finally, she allowed herself to be led away down the hallway.

The silver spoon still rested between the bricks. The only proof that Doxie had that anyone had ever loved her.

PART III

CHAPTER 10

Four Years Later

BREAKFAST in the workhouse was less of a meal and more a subdued but intense battle of wills.

Doxie could feel the tension rising around her now, as she stood in line in front of one of the two long tables at the far end of the room. Each was staffed by a grim-faced woman; they had survived the workhouse themselves and were employed now to help care – for want of a better word – for the children. Doxie knew from experience that they wielded ladles like weapons.

She trembled slightly, staring at the two gigantic, steaming pots standing on the tables. They contained something plain, she knew – gruel or porridge – but her stomach was aching for food. The workhouse provided three meals a day—if one could keep them from being eaten by someone else.

The line moved a step forward. Doxie held her breath. She had reached the spot where one picked up a bent tin bowl from the table. She took one, careful to hold it up in front of her so that the ladies wouldn't think that she'd taken more than one.

A few more steps forward, and Doxie was holding out her bowl for the glob of porridge to be dropped into the bottom. It burned her fingers slightly, but the feeling was good, for the workhouse was a frigid building in December.

The next part was the dangerous one. Clutching her tin bowl and spoon, Doxie hurried toward one of the tables where rows upon rows of girls were sitting. The table right in the back was always the one to avoid; that was where the bullies and troublemakers sat. Right in the front was best, but it was usually taken by all the tiniest girls, and Doxie didn't have the heart to take their place.

With her heart in her mouth, Doxie hastened toward the second table. She could see from the corner of her eye that one of the bigger girls was right behind her, and Doxie knew that she would do whatever it took to get Doxie's plate from her – if Doxie was unlucky enough to sit where the ladies at the main table couldn't easily see them.

There was one spot left at the second table, the safe one. Doxie lengthened her stride, walking frantically; running wasn't allowed in the dining hall. The other girl was bigger, her legs longer, and she was breathing right down Doxie's neck. If she took that spot –

Doxie made it, barely. She threw herself onto the bench, clinging to her plate, and started eating in massive gulps, shovelling the scalding porridge into her mouth. This time, she'd been lucky. The other girl passed by, throwing a last, scathing glance over her shoulder, and Doxie breathed a tiny sigh of relief.

Her mouth was burning, but at least she had her breakfast to herself. It was getting easier now that she was among the older girls in this group. In the early days, she had hardly ever finished a whole meal.

She slowed down now, eating a little more calmly. Almost of its own accord, her hand reached into her pocket and gently caressed the spoon that rested there. She remembered so vividly how empty the pocket of her workhouse dress had felt on that first night, as she shared a bunk with a stranger and lay listening to the breathing of the other girls in the dark. She still didn't know how she'd been able to sneak out of the dormitory, head to the intake room, and retrieve her spoon from its spot between the bricks. Another little miracle, perhaps. It felt as though this spoon was the only miracle she had left.

"Attention!" called a stern voice from the front of the dining hall.

Doxie sat up straighter, a cold stab of fear running through her. That voice belonged to the one person she feared more than anyone else in the world: the matron, Mrs. Fickling. In terms of ferocity, coldness, and sheer harshness, she put even Mrs. Boggs and Miss Peggy to shame.

Utter silence fell on the dining hall. Mrs. Fickling swept them all with an icy gaze that ran over them like a cold wind on an open field, frosting everything in its path. Then she spoke.

"Doxie Shaw," she said. "Megan Biggles. Stand up."

Doxie rose to her feet, her knees trembling; so did the other girl, one of the small ones at the first table.

"Come here," ordered Mrs. Fickling.

Doxie felt sick. Had Mrs. Fickling found out about the spoon? What would the punishment be for the gross transgression of holding onto something she loved? She thought of the refractory ward, the dark and silent cell where girls could be confined for as long as three days, all alone in the darkness. She herself had never been inside, but she'd heard terrifying stories. Would she be whipped instead?

Praying for a mere whipping, Doxie shuffled across to Mrs. Fickling, the other little girl right behind her. She dared not look at the matron's face. Instead, she stared down at her feet. One was tapping impatiently.

"Yes, ma'am," she breathed.

"Did I speak to you, Miss Shaw?" snapped Mrs. Fickling.

Doxie was silent.

"Answer me!" roared Mrs. Fickling.

"I don't know, ma'am!" Doxie yelped, terrified.

"Are you deaf as well as stupid, child?" snapped Mrs. Fickling. She drew back her hand, and Doxie cowered, bracing herself for the blow; but it never came. Instead, Mrs. Fickling let out an angry sigh and dropped her hand to her side. "Can't have you going out with bruises on your face," she muttered. "Miss Shaw, Miss Biggles, you have been hired."

Doxie felt dismay fill her heart. She'd been hired out for the first time when she was ten years old, shortly after coming to the workhouse. When manor houses needed an extra hand for a season, they'd hire a child from the workhouse. Some girls told stories about kind mistresses who'd given them extra food or bits of clothing – even though the clothing was confiscated when they returned to the workhouse. But Doxie's experiences had never been pleasant.

"Well, don't just stand there," snapped Mrs. Fickling. "Ellen will be walking you to the manor immediately after breakfast, Miss Shaw. I suggest you return to your table and make haste. As for you, Miss Biggles, you will leave after lunch."

"Yes, ma'am. Thank you, ma'am," Doxie mumbled.

She walked back to her table on numb legs, knowing that her bowl had long since been cleaned out behind her back, and dreading what this Christmas season might bring.

***

Doxie first began to hope a little when she laid eyes on the manor house.

The previous houses where she had worked had all been as stern and imposing as castles, rising up against the sky like monuments to their owners' cold hearts. This one, however, had a hint of warmth around it. It had pillars and eaves and gables just like the other houses, and it, too, loomed up among the surrounding trees; but when Doxie followed Miss Ellen, one of the stern-faced workhouse ladies, up the path to the servants' entrance, she saw that this manor house had an orchard. The trees were all bare and black against the snow now, but there was a swing hanging from the lowest branch of one gnarled old apple tree. There were children here.

Besides the swing, there was something a little softer and more rounded about this place. When they passed by the stable block, there was a light trap standing in the yard instead of an elaborate coach, and a pair of cats were sunning themselves on the wall. Chickens scattered around Doxie's feet as they reached the narrow back door. Their clucks were homely and reminded Doxie of the orphanage's little farmyard and of Owen.

The thought gave her the courage she needed to stand up straight, hands behind her back, as Ellen knocked on the door. It swung open, and an amazingly short woman in a white apron glared up at Ellen.

"What do you want?" she demanded.

"Payment," snapped Ellen. "I'm from the workhouse. I've brought you a scullery-maid."

The cook looked at Doxie, who felt very small and out of place in the oversized black-and-white uniform that the workhouse had dressed her in. The woman's eyes softened just a little.

"Very well," she said. "I'll call the housekeeper; she'll bring you the money." She turned to Doxie. "Come along then, child."

"Yes, ma'am," said Doxie, stepping through the door and into a vast kitchen that clanged with activity. Cleaning, boiling, roasting, frying, washing – an army of people in black-and-white uniforms was swarming through the big room. The cook gestured at a huge sink heaped with everything from china to pots and pans.

"There you are, pet," she said, her tone a little softer now. "Have at it."

"Yes, ma'am," said Doxie.

The cook gave her a steady look. "You needn't be afraid," she said. "If you work hard, we'll treat you well. What's your name?"

"Doxie," she said.

"Very well then, Doxie. Do your work with a good heart, and you'll be all right."

The cook bustled off, and Doxie stepped up to the giant stack of dishes. Maybe things might be a little better here after all.

CHAPTER 11

WYLIE MANOR HAD HIRED Doxie for seven days, and by the third day, she was already wishing that she never had to go back to the workhouse.

Her taskmaster was the cook, Mrs. Cromwell, who insisted that Doxie call her Patty. Even though she never stood still for more than fifteen seconds together, Patty was kind enough in her own way. Doxie slept warmly in the servants' quarters on a bunk of her own and ate three hot meals a day without the threat of having her food stolen by other ravenous girls. It was more than she had ever had before, and even though the work was unceasing – Mrs. Wylie was hosting an enormous Christmas party in a few days' time – Doxie was more or less happy for the first time in many years.

Her main task was washing dishes, and truth be told, her arms did ache with exhaustion by the time she had finished with the lunch dishes – and that was before she had to face the mountain of dirty dishes the Wylie family always generated at supper. They were cramping now as she ran one plate after the other through the rinse water, stacking them on the draining board, moving carefully to avoid so much as chipping the edge of one of these plates.

Finally, the last of the plates were done. She stepped back, stretching her sore arms. As if summoned, Mrs. Cromwell appeared in the doorway of the scullery.

"Done with the dishes, are you?" she said.

"Yes, ma'am," said Doxie.

"Good. Take out the rubbish, then," she said, "and hurry back. The stove isn't going to polish itself before dinner, you know."

"Yes, ma'am." Doxie shook out her aching arms and headed over to the garbage can in the corner of the scullery. At least this one was on wheels, unlike the heavy ones at the workhouse, which she had to drag across the ground. Tipping it onto its end, she pulled it across the kitchen floor with a deafening rattle and headed out of the servant's entrance and into a crisply cold day.

It was a perfect day, despite the frigid air that nipped at Doxie's fingers and made her breath a plume of steam. The long lawns were all covered in snow, and it glittered in the pale sunlight that filtered down from a sky so pale blue that it felt like being inside some cold jewel. Doxie took deep breaths of the comparatively fresh air, almost wishing she could stay on as a maid here at Wylie Manor forever. But the Wylies didn't need more help. They just needed a little workhouse girl to help them for the Christmas party.

Happy giggling floated to Doxie on the breeze. She had just passed the stable yard, and she looked to her left, where the laughter was coming from the lovely old orchard. A very fat chestnut pony was trotting gamely through the snow, dragging a little sleigh, its fine bells jingling on his harness. The pony was a cheerful little thing with a bushy forelock and tiny triangular ears, and Doxie had to pause to admire him. Two little girls – the Wylie sisters – were sitting in the sleigh, driving the pony, and their giggling was beautiful even though Doxie had to work hard not to feel envious of their warm clothes.

"Careful!" called a joyously familiar young male voice.

Doxie stopped dead in her tracks. Surely... no. It couldn't be. She was imagining things.

The girls gave a squeal of alarm. They had failed to turn the pony tightly enough, and one runner of the sleigh ground to a halt on an exposed tree-root.

"It's all right!" laughed that same beloved voice, and this time Doxie was sure she wasn't imagining it, because he walked out from behind one of the bigger trees, laughing and smiling in a way that struck joy right into the pit of Doxie's belly.

Somehow, wonderfully, inexplicably, it was Owen.

She stood rooted to the spot, unable to move or breathe as he strode up to the little girls' sleigh. He was laughing right along with them, talking with them the way he used to talk with the little children back at the orphanage. Doxie could have stood there for hours, just listening to his sweet voice.

Budging the sleigh from the root, he straightened up and gave the pony an affectionate slap on the rump. "There you are, girls!" he said. "Try again. And remember that the sleigh turns wider than he does, this time."

Chortling with laughter, the girls set off once more, driving the pony in swooping arcs around the trees. Owen laughed, watching them. They passed by between him and Doxie, and somehow his eyes went from watching the pony to suddenly locking onto her.

She saw him freeze. She, too, was frozen, garbage can in hand, simply staring.

His voice was shaky when he called to the girls next. "Just keep away from the trees," he said. "I... I'll be right over here."

He stumbled toward her, climbing through the rail fence of the orchard, his feet ungainly in the thick snow. Stopping a few yards from her, he just stared for a few moments, his hands hanging limply by his sides.

Doxie wanted to stop time and speed it up all at once.

He spoke first. "D-Doxie?" he breathed.

"Owen." Up until that moment, she had half believed that it was a dream, but when he said her name, she knew it was real. "Oh, Owen!" she gasped, letting go of the garbage can.

He rushed to her, throwing his arms around her in a brief and clumsy but sincere embrace. "I can't believe it's you!" he cried, stepping back, and thrusting his hands into his pockets.

"Neither can I," Doxie cried, laughing and crying at the same time. "It seems so unreal. It's been so long."

"Nearly five years," said Owen. "Miss Peggy kept saying you were a no-good thief, but I knew it wasn't true."

"I stole a photograph, Owen," said Doxie. "That little baby that came the day before I left – she had a photograph of her parents tucked into her blankets. I took it to keep it safe."

"I knew it would be something like that." Owen beamed. "I was so worried about you. So afraid for you."

"And I for you," said Doxie. She shuddered. "I was so afraid you'd been sent to work in a factory... or to become a chimney-sweep."

"It was nothing like that. I work here for the Wylies now," said Owen. "The orphanage sent me here to be a stable-boy, just as I'd hoped. And I love it here. The little girls are lovely. The people are good, and they treat me fairly, even though the stablemaster has me work from dawn to dusk."

"Mrs. Cromwell in the kitchen is the same," said Doxie. "She doesn't let me stop for a minute, but she's kind in her own stern way."

"That's good." Owen laughed with joy. "I can't believe you're working here now, too. We can see each other all the time. It'll be so good to have a friend working here."

Doxie felt her heart break within her. "Yes... we can," she sighed, reality suddenly reappearing like a bucket of cold water over her head. "But only for a few more days."

"A few more days?" Owen's face filled with dismay. "What do you mean?"

"I'm... I'm not in a permanent position here." Doxie hung her head. "I'm on hire from the workhouse."

"The workhouse?" Owen's face fell. "Oh, Doxie... I'm so sorry." He seemed to be taking in her thin limbs and pinched face for the first time. "I... I wish there was something I could do."

"So do I." Doxie hung her head. "I have to go back to the workhouse on Wednesday. But Mrs. Cromwell said that Mrs. Wylie is holding a New Year's party in two weeks' time, too.

Perhaps she'll hire me again then. Mrs. Cromwell said I work hard, and she'd ask the housekeeper to arrange for me to come again for a few days then."

"That's wonderful." Owen beamed. "I'll see you then. And maybe... well, maybe I can come up with a way to keep you out of the workhouse by that time."

"What?" gasped Doxie. "How?"

"I don't know. But there are plenty of manor houses around here. Someone must be looking for a maid," said Owen. "I'll ask round. I'm sure Mrs. Cromwell will help me, too."

"Oh, Owen..." Doxie's eyes filled with tears. "Thank you. No one... no one has really wanted to help me in a very long time. Thank you."

"Of course, Doxie," said Owen. "You've always been my best friend."

"Doxie!"

The shout shattered the peace in which Doxie and Owen had existed for a few precious moments. Doxie spun around to see Mrs. Cromwell standing in the kitchen doorway.

"Hurry up, child!" she shouted. "The stove needs polishing. Time's wasting! Get moving!"

"I'd better go," said Doxie.

"Me too. The stablemaster will be angry if he sees me standing around," admitted Owen. "But we'll see each other after work, perhaps for a few moments."

"Yes," said Doxie. "Perhaps."

She hurried away, even though purposefully walking away from her only friend in the world was a terrible wrench. But his promise rang in her ears – and so did his words, telling her that she had always been his best friend.

She reached into her pocket, ran her fingers over the silver spoon. These tiny scraps of evidence that she still meant something to someone were the only sustenance her soul really had.

CHAPTER 12

CHAOS RESOUNDED all around Doxie as she cowered in a corner with the smallest children, trying in vain to see past the nest of heads and arms and legs between her corner and the blackboard on the far side of the room. The lesson always seemed to be the same thing; most of the children here never moved far past the alphabet. In four years of lessons, Doxie had barely managed to piece together a few sounds and a tiny bit of reading.

"It's no use," sighed Sarah, one of the smallest girls. She angrily threw down her slate pencil. "I can't see anything on the board."

"Why should we even try?" demanded Daphne, another little girl. She looked up at Doxie, her eyes hollow. "I'm so hungry and tired. I just want to sleep. No one else is paying any attention, so why should we?"

Doxie bit her lip. Daphne's words were absolutely true. The other girls, almost without exception, were talking constantly among each other. The bigger girls' coarse laughter and conversation almost completely drowned out the voice of the teacher; a tiny, wispy woman with a puny voice. She would have had trouble making herself heard in a quiet nursery with two well-behaved children. Here, in this cavernous room with nearly fifty girls, her task was hopeless, and she knew it.

"Daphne's right. It's no use," said Sarah.h

Doxie reached out, gathering the two smaller girls into her arms. They were so tiny, so bony; their ribs and shoulder bones pressed harshly into Doxie's arms.

"We have to learn to read, girls," she said softly, hoping that her embrace would mean something to them. She closed her eyes, trying not to think of Daffy and Tulip and Posy, of how wonderful it had been to see their smiling faces and hold them in her arms. She thought of Trudy and of the babies back at the orphanage, and her heart ached with not knowing how any of them were.

"But why?" asked Sarah on a hopeless sigh.

"Because one day, being able to read might give us all a better future," said Doxie. "One where we can get good work and make something of ourselves." Those were the words that

Mrs. Boggs had always used in the orphanage, on the rare occasions that she bothered to try to teach the children anything; invariably, it had ended in lost tempers and frayed nerves.

"A better future!" Daphne shook her head. "There's no future, Doxie. There's only this workhouse."

Doxie cuddled both girls a little closer, hoping somehow to find the strength to believe that Daphne's words weren't true, that somehow they would find a way out of this cold and dreary place.

Her heart thumped twice as she thought of Owen's promise, made to her one week ago. He was going to try to find a way for her to be free, for them to be able to see one another.

He was her better future – and she trusted him with helping her.

※

DOXIE WAS IN A NURSERY. It was unlike anything she'd seen before, but it seemed to be like the kind of room she'd heard other girls in the workhouse describing, girls who had worked as parlor-maids before or even once had a nursery to call their own before hard times destroyed their families. All the things they'd talked about were in here: the thick, navy blue carpeting on the floor; the crackling hearth fire, filling the room with warmth and dancing golden light; the colourful throw rug by the fireplace; the bed with elegant iron posts and thick covers. There were toys, too, dolls on the ground, books on the shelves, a perfect dapple-grey rocking-horse in the back corner.

Doxie found it a little strange that there were dolls and a rocking-horse here in this room, in her room. She knew somehow that this was her own nursery, even though she'd never actually been inside one, but surely, she was too old for these kind of toys. She was drawn to the books instead. Floating over to the shelf, she pulled one down, opening it. It was full of bright pictures and colours and words, although Doxie couldn't quite seem to see any of them clearly, but she knew that they were all beautiful and lovely.

There was a rocking noise coming from the corner. She turned to see the rocking-horse coming toward her, swaying back and forth, his soft black mane and tail rippling with the movement. Putting out her hand, she touched his smooth nose, with the perfectly painted nostrils flaring against her fingers.

She smiled at it. "Good old rocking-horse," she said.

The rocking-horse said something. It sounded like a name, but it wasn't "Doxie"; yet she could feel that it was her own name somehow.

"What?" she asked.

Then it began to warp under her hand. Its pretty dapples turned waxy and melted; the blackness of the mane and tail shrunk away, and the entire form began to morph, rippling and changing like something liquid.

Doxie screamed. Staggering backwards, she found herself pressed up against the bookshelves as the rocking-horse changed. There was a strange, ethereal whinny from within its changing form, and then, suddenly, it was a spoon. Just a small spoon lying on the carpet, glittering slightly.

Doxie padded across the carpet, holding her breath, and she knew the spoon at once. It was her silver spoon, the one she always carried with her. She bent down hastily and snatched it up, tracing her thumb over the floral engraving on the end.

"What was that you were saying?" she whispered, holding the spoon up to her face. "What was it? What was it? What was it?"

The urgency of her whispers surrounded her, spinning her around like a breeze, lifting her feet from the floor of the nursery until she was twirled around and around in the question. She clung to the spoon, but everything was spinning, and suddenly the wind disappeared from under her form, and she was falling –

Doxie sat up, gasping, in total darkness. Around her, she could hear the deep breathing of sleeping girls; two small figures were curled up against her, and a threadbare blanket made from sacking was sliding down to her knees.

She was in the workhouse dormitory, right where she belonged.

There was a whimper from one of the other little girls sharing the tiny bunk with her, and Doxie lay back down again, tugging the blanket more tightly around the three of them. She reached into her pocket, her fingers finding the spoon. This wasn't the first time she'd had a strange dream about it.

She couldn't forget the rocking-horse or the word it had whispered to her before it began to change.

She knew she could never admit it to anyone, or she would be a candidate for Bedlam itself. But in that dream, it had felt like the spoon was trying to tell her something.

"GINA, PLEASE," Doxie begged, spreading her arms to protect the row of little girls cowering on the bench behind her. "Please, just leave them alone."

Gina was one of the oldest girls in the workhouse. She had been raised here, likely even born within these austere walls—she didn't know, and no one had ever told her. Nearly fourteen years of hardship in this place had toughened every part of the girl to unyielding steel: the bones of her hands that flexed against her skin as she balled them into fists; the harsh lines of her high cheekbones and protruding eye sockets; the icy look in her pale green eyes.

"You don't want to do this, pest," she snapped. "Get out of my way."

"Please, Gina, they're hungry." Doxie swallowed hard. She never liked confronting the bullies, but she'd seen Gina steal entire meals from the three little girls behind her for days in a row. She knew that those children were starving. "You've had your portion. Let them have theirs."

"Get out of the way!" Gina raised her fists.

Doxie glanced desperately toward the long tables at the top of the room. The women who served their meals had taken their pots back to the kitchens; if Gina was going to pick a fight, she'd have free rein for several minutes before they returned. Looking at the taller, angry girl, Doxie knew that she didn't stand a chance.

But every minute that Gina spent shouting at her or fighting her was a minute longer that the little girls could eat. That made it worth her while. She closed her own fists, tipping up her chin.

"I don't want to fight you," she said, "but I will, if I have to."

Gina cackled bitterly. "You don't have to," she said. "You're just stupid." She advanced a step, drawing back one of her bony little fists, her teeth bared in a grimace of terrifying rage –

"Attention!"

Never before had Doxie been so relieved to hear the dreaded voice of Mrs. Fickling. Immediately, Gina spun around, her hands behind her back. Like every other girl in the dining hall, she knew better than to give Mrs. Fickling anything but her full attention when that frightening word resounded through the big room.

The fact that Mrs. Fickling had stopped Gina from giving Doxie a good punching wasn't the only reason why Doxie was glad to see her. It was two weeks after she'd left Wylie Manor, and she knew that Mrs. Fickling's presence in the dining hall meant just one thing: Mrs. Cromwell had made good on her promise, and Doxie was going back to Wylie Manor. She was going to see Owen again. Her heart took wing at the thought. Even though it had always been cold and dark by the time they both finished working, they had spent some happy hours sitting on the wall of the stable yard and talking. They were the happiest times that Doxie could remember. And Owen had said he would find a way to get her out of the workhouse.

Owen had said he would try to set her free, and she trusted him. Even now, he must be waiting in the stable yard with eager anticipation, glancing toward the servants' entrance from time to time, waiting for Doxie to come to Wylie Manor.

Heart thudding with excitement, Doxie couldn't help grinning as she watched Mrs. Fickling. As usual, the matron gave the girls all a long and bitter glance before speaking.

"Annie Cooper!" she snapped. "Linda Rogan!" There was an interminable pause, and Doxie's heart felt that it would stop in her chest, then, "Doxie Shaw!"

Breathing a sigh of relief, Doxie slipped out from behind Gina and walked up to Mrs. Fickling, the other two girls close behind her. She made sure not to look up at Mrs. Fickling's face, but this time her tremors were from excitement instead of fear. Remembering Mrs. Fickling's anger last time, she was completely silent as she stood in front of the manor.

"Well?" snapped Mrs. Fickling. "Are you dumb as well as stupid, child?"

Doxie stared up at her in disbelief.

"I'm speaking to you!" Mrs. Fickling shouted. "Answer me!"

Her anger was like sleet driven on a strong wind, sending cold and shock through Doxie's body as it drove against her. What had she done to anger the matron this time? But she wouldn't show her fear. Not this time. Soon, she would never have to face Mrs. Fickling again.

"Yes, ma'am," she said.

Mrs. Fickling's eyes narrowed, but she turned away from Doxie and glared at the two other girls instead. "Miss Cooper, Miss Rogan, Miss Shaw, you've been hired."

Shudders ran through the girls; Doxie's was from pure excitement. She couldn't wait to walk away from this terrible place forever.

"Miss Cooper, you'll be going to the millinery down the street. Their girl is sick, and they need a replacement for a few weeks until she recovers." Mrs. Fickling turned to the other girl. "Miss Rogan, you'll be going to Wylie Manor."

The words sent a jolt of ice down Doxie's spine. Wylie Manor? Perhaps Mrs. Cromwell needed two assistants for this party. The alternative was unthinkable.

She felt herself shaking, in true fear this time, as Mrs. Fickling turned to face her.

"You, Miss Shaw," she said abruptly, "will be going to the other side of London; a fishmonger there needs a shop assistant on the docks."

"The docks!" Doxie cried. Horror shot through her. A fishmonger's assistant – and all the way on the other side of London! How would she ever find Owen now?

"You'll be gone just for the day. You'll return here tonight," said Mrs. Fickling. "Come and wash up. There's no time to waste."

The other two girls hurried toward the door with trembling obedience, but Doxie couldn't seem to bring her feet to move. She stood rooted to the spot, shaking from head to toe. How had this happened?

"Come on, child," snapped Mrs. Fickling.

Doxie stared into her eyes. There was only one thing she feared more at this moment than confronting Mrs. Fickling, and it was spending the day in a smelly fish shop, dealing with some angry fishmonger, and then returning back to this dreadful place. She had hoped that this would be her last meal in the workhouse dining hall. No, she had *believed* that this would be the last one, and now it felt as though the very breath had been snatched from her lungs.

"Please, ma'am," she stammered out. "Mrs. Cromwell said she'd ask for me to return to Wylie Manor for their party."

Mrs. Fickling's eyes narrowed. "Are you contradicting my orders, child?" she hissed.

"No, ma'am," Doxie quavered. "I... I just think there's... there's been a mistake."

"A mistake!" Mrs. Fickling reared back, her eyes filling with venom. "You dare accuse *me* of a mistake?" she roared.

Doxie knew the blow was coming, and that to dodge it would be useless. She stood for it, cringing, and sure enough Mrs. Fickling's hand came down on Doxie's cheekbone with a force that knocked the breath from her. Her mouth filled with blood, and she staggered back, careful not to cry out in pain lest it would earn her another stunning blow.

"No mistake has been made, you ungrateful and insolent child," Mrs. Fickling snapped. "Mrs. Cromwell can request whatever she pleases; your fates are in my hands, and mine alone. You will not be going to cosy Wylie Manor, no matter what you or that foolish old crone would want. You will be going to the fishmonger's, like I told you." Her eyes narrowed. "Or to the refractory ward."

Doxie felt tears streaming down her cheeks, mingling with blood from her wounded lip. She wanted to scream. She wanted to throw herself at Mrs. Fickling and claw at her face and roar that it was unfair, that she couldn't take away the only hope that Doxie had simply out of petty spite.

But she knew that Mrs. Fickling had already done just that. There was no fighting it. There would be no argument.

"Well?" hissed the older woman. "What do you say to that, you stupid child?"

Doxie hung her head and spoke the only words she knew that would keep her from the unthinkable fate of the refractory ward.

"Yes, ma'am," she mumbled.

CHAPTER 13

TEARS POURED down Doxie's cheeks as she sat in the back corner of the classroom. She could feel them coursing down her skin, hot and wet as blood, but she made no move to reach up and wipe them away.

Why would she? They had been flowing almost continuously ever since Mrs. Fickling told her that she wasn't going back to Wylie Manor. In fact, Doxie was sure now that she would never go back to the manor, ever again. Not if Mrs. Fickling had anything to do with it.

The fishmonger had been cruel. He'd slapped her with a dead fish when she had failed to work quickly enough for his liking, and she could feel the tears running over the tender place on her cheekbone where Mrs. Fickling had struck her, too. Yet she would rather had been beaten to a pulp than to suffer the feeling she had now, a feeling that she had always seemed to hold at bay until now: absolute hopelessness.

Around Doxie, chaos reigned. Girls were shouting, fighting, playing, and generally ignoring the teacher who cowered by the side of her blackboard, stammering out words and sounds as she pointed at the letters that she wrote there every morning. They were almost always the same ones; they never seemed to get very far. The only girls who weren't completely ignoring the teacher's presence were Gina and the other bigger girls. Instead of paying attention, these were pelting her with bits of chalk and their slate pencils, and the teacher cried out for them to stop.

It didn't matter, then, that Doxie was sitting motionless in the back of the room with her slate lying in her lap, untouched, its black surface empty. The teacher had bigger problems than just a crying girl in the back of the room.

There was a tug at Doxie's sleeve. She pulled her arm away, annoyed; she simply wanted to be left alone. It was the only grace anyone could give her now, the only thing that she dared to expect from another human being.

The tug came again. "Doxie?" said a small voice.

Doxie felt a piece of herself melting. She looked down into Daphne and Sarah's upturned faces. They were clutching their slates, a poor attempt at the letter A scrawled on each one, and their eyes were pleading.

"Please, Doxie," piped little Sarah. "Help us to learn."

"It's so sad to see you cry," said Daphne. She sat down close beside Doxie, cuddling her little head against Doxie's side. "We love it when you smile. We need you."

Doxie felt something inside her shattering. She reached out, drawing both the small girls into her lap, burying her face in their unwashed hair, holding them both as tightly as she could.

She realised then that she needed them as much as they needed her. If the workhouse was her fate forever, and she would never look into Owen's eyes again, then caring for these little ones was all she had left.

Doxie took a deep, shaky breath. Setting down the little girls, she managed a smile and wiped her eyes.

"All right, then," she said. "Show me your slates."

A HAUNTING melody rang through the dark woods as Doxie walked beneath the soaring boughs of the old pine trees. She knew the song, yet she couldn't quite remember the words. There was absolutely no other sound in this great old forest. Her feet were silent on the damp earth, and if there was any wind – and it seemed that there must be, for the branches stirred slightly high above her – then it wasn't causing even the faintest rustle in the branches.

Doxie trailed her fingertips over the rough bark of the nearest tree as she walked. She wasn't sure where she was going, but she knew that she had to get there somehow, and she kept on walking even as the trees grew thicker.

The melody, too, was growing louder and louder. She paused in a small clearing, littered with luminescent purple flowers the likes of which Doxie had never seen before. Listening, she realised at last that she recognised that song. It was the same one she sang to Daphne and Sarah every night to get them to sleep.

Home! Home! Sweet, sweet home!

Doxie knew she was singing along, even though she could only hear the distant melody, not the words she sang herself. Pushing forward, she broke through the clearing into another: a wide and dappled glade, with a splashing stream running through it. That was where it was waiting for her. The spoon. It lay shimmering on a rock by the water, and Doxie knew that the music was coming from it somehow.

The second stanza. The one she'd always made up. She knew that the spoon knew it, that if she just grasped it and held it up to her ear, she would finally hear the last stanza of *Home, Sweet Home*. She would know at last the meaning of that beautiful and mysterious word.

Doxie stepped forward, and a roar tore the peaceful silence. Whirling around, she saw it. A great, shadowy monster, all horns and claws and red, glowing eyes, and dripping yellow fangs that flashed as it roared again. It wore Mrs. Fickling's spectacles.

And it was coming for her.

Doxie screamed, lunging toward the spoon. But the faster she ran, the further it was from her, the longer the glade grew. The spoon was shooting away from her, growing smaller and smaller, the distance yawning between them until it was little more than a silver glimmer on the horizon. Doxie shrieked, but it was no use. And the monster was getting closer and closer. She could feel its claws wrapping around her legs...

She woke, gasping, trembling in the darkness, tears of horror coursing down her cheeks. The beautiful woods were gone. There was nothing here except silence and darkness, and the sounds of the other girls sleeping all around her, angry mutters from the bunks next to her as disgruntled sleepers tried to get back to bed.

Doxie closed her eyes, cuddling a little further down into her blankets. She closed her hand around the spoon, but no words came to her.

The melody of home was still a secret to her.

PART IV

CHAPTER 14

Four Years Later

DOXIE STARED WISTFULLY through the iron bars of the work yard's gate. Here, there was nothing but stone paving and summer sun, pounding down mercilessly on the backs and necks of the women who sat bent over their work. They were picking oakum – using blunt nails to tease out individual strands from old ropes, to be used later for caulking – and the work was exhausting. Doxie's back and hips ached constantly from sitting on the stone, her legs folded underneath her. Her fingers stung from the effort of picking out the fibres, and her skin was dry and chafed from the rough textures.

She knew that every other woman in the work yard was suffering just as she was, perhaps more. Some of them were little more than girls, only fourteen or fifteen years old, and they struggled with the difficult work, yet they were still expected to meet the same quota. Others were aged, their hair white, their faces as deeply lined as the ropes themselves, their fingers all askew and gnarled with overwork. They, too, were expected to work as tirelessly as far younger women.

There was nothing here in this bare yard except for suffering women with sore fingers and aching backs and broken hearts. For three long years – ever since Mrs. Fickling had decided that Doxie must be fourteen now and had moved her forcibly into the women's group – Doxie had been spending every day in this yard with these women and the oakum. And there was only one thing that could keep her heart alive in this hard time: the view through the iron gate into the little girls' exercise yard.

She had learned the hard way that to get up and walk across to the gate, or even to call out the name of a girl she recognised in that yard, would earn her a beating or a night in the refractory ward. Mrs. Fickling believed that being in the workhouse meant relinquishing one's right to human connection. All Doxie could do was to stare through the gate, her practiced fingers tearing at the ropes of their own according, watching the girls out there in the yard as they played or just sat in unhappy heaps, suffering through a few more hours before lunchtime and what meagre sustenance they would be afforded.

She could see Daphne and Sarah, still fast friends, sitting off to one side on their own. Even though they were no longer the smallest children, they were still only about eight or nine years old, and that left them terrifyingly vulnerable to the other bullies. Doxie had been praying ever since she left the girls' group that someone would take them under her wing and look after them the way she had done.

So far, those prayers had gone unanswered, and Doxie was particularly worried about Annie Cooper. She was one of the oldest girls, and she'd been sweet enough a few years ago. But these days, toughness was coming into her words and movements. She was growing as hard and cold as all the other girls who survived the workhouse for too long.

There were days when Doxie feared that coldness more than any other fate.

"Ma'am," cried a raucous and horribly familiar voice.

Doxie jumped, knowing instantly what was coming. She ducked her head, turning her full attention back to the length of rope in her hands. Twisting at it frantically, digging at it with the blunt nail, she struggled to wrestle a few more fibres free, to look as busy as possible.

"Ma'am," called Gina's voice again, making Doxie's stomach twist in worry. "Look at that Doxie girl. She's hardly done a thing all morning!"

Doxie felt the palms of her hands beginning to sweat. Trembling, she continued to work as fast as she could, holding her breath. Gina's words were untrue; the heap of fibres by her side was the same size as some of the other girls'. Bigger than Gina's, she knew. Gina had somehow wormed her way into their supervisor's good graces, and she spent a lot of her time chatting with the two girls who followed her around like faithful dogs, rather than picking oakum.

The dread tramp of approaching feet drew nearer to Doxie. She continued to work frantically, knowing that Gina was sitting just a few yards away from her.

"What did you say, Miss Rose?" asked the supervisor.

Doxie knew that there would be a sneer on Gina's face; she didn't have to look up to see it. When Gina was moved to the women's group, Doxie had hoped never to see her again, only to join that same group a year later.

"I've been watching Doxie Shaw," said Gina's nasal voice. "She's been sitting there staring at nothing rather than working. It's been going on all morning."

There were a few moments of silence. Doxie's hands trembled, and she dropped the nail, then fumbled to take it back again.

The footsteps drew closer. Doxie didn't have to look up to know that Mrs. Gantry, the muscular woman appointed to supervise the workhouse women as they worked, was standing right behind her.

"What do you have to say for yourself, Doxie Shaw?" sneered Mrs. Gantry.

"N-nothing, ma'am," Doxie stammered out.

Mrs. Gantry impaled Doxie with an icy glance that she felt between her shoulder blades like a thrown knife, and Doxie could do little other than tremble. The woman leaned down a little and peered at the heap of oakum lying beside her. Doxie's fingers were flying over the rope, slick and clumsy with sweat and nerves, and she could only hope that Mrs. Gantry wouldn't find fault with her.

Eventually, the harsh woman straightened. "Very well," she said. "I can't fault you this time, Shaw, but you mark my words – I know you're a lazy one." Her voice deepened, growing ominous. "Mrs. Fickling won't easily forget your defiance, and she will never forgive it. Think on that next time you decide to push your boundaries."

Doxie didn't breathe until Mrs. Gantry's trim footsteps had walked away. Just as she began to relax, Gina leaned closer and spat. The disgusting glob of transparent slime slapped into the ground right by Doxie's feet.

"I'm watching you," she hissed.

Gina strode away, and Doxie let out her breath slowly and shakily to avoid bursting into tears.

The tears covered her eyes with a glassy film, and she blinked at them as she continued to work. If only Mrs. Fickling had never been so spiteful. Then she could have gone to Wylie Manor, to Owen, and he would have found a way for her to be free.

It broke her heart to think of him in that stable yard, glancing constantly at the kitchens as he worked, waiting and waiting for Doxie to come. She ached to imagine his confusion and sorrow when the girl who arrived in an oversized maid's uniform wasn't Doxie at all. She wondered if he still thought about her all these years later, if he still wondered where she was and how she was doing.

If he still thought of her as the best friend he'd ever had.

Her heart had long since shattered; Doxie felt as though it had been ripped in two by all the loss she had experienced. Yet each time she thought of gentle Owen, and of what might have been if she'd only been able to go back to Wylie Manor for that New Year's party, it felt as though the old wound was torn open a little wider.

※

THERE WERE two occasions every day during which Doxie was tantalizingly close to her treasured Daphne and Sarah. That was when she was in the work yard and the children were in the neighbouring exercise yard, just through that wrought-iron gate; and again in the evenings, when the children had just finished their meal and left the dining hall down the south hallway, while the women were entering through the north hallway.

Doxie always tried to be at the front of the line for this, although it was difficult when there were older women – women who were quicker with their elbows, and sharp with both their tongues and their slaps – who wanted to crowd into the dining hall and get to the food before she could.

On this day, she had made it a few yards from the very front of the row. Her heart was pounding as she waited for the door to open so that she and the other women could go into the dining hall. Even though her stomach growled for the watery soup or hard bread that awaited them for lunch, there was something else she longed for even more: to see Daphne and Sarah.

Finally, the door swung open, and even before she could step into the dining hall, she knew they were in trouble.

A shrill voice resounded through the cavernous room. A little girl was screeching at the top of her lungs, and her shrieks radiated terror. And someone else was shouting, too, shouting and sobbing.

That voice was horrifyingly familiar. It was Sarah.

For once, Doxie shoved aside the other women as she burst into the dining hall, and a scene of chaos lay before her. Annie Cooper was standing with her hands raised, towering over

Daphne, who lay on the ground, crying wholeheartedly. The bigger girl held a tin bowl in her hands, a dent marking the place where she'd brought it smashing down upon the temple of little Daphne, who was weeping and clutching her head. Sarah was a few yards away, her hands clasped over her mouth, screaming in terror.

"Daphne!" Doxie cried, rushing forward, but she only ran a few yards before freezing in her tracks. Mrs. Fickling had burst in through the south door, and instead of looking at Daphne – who was now staggering to her feet, hands clasped to her head – her eyes were fixed upon Doxie.

She knew that to take one more step would be to anger the matron beyond expression.

"No!" Sarah squealed.

Doxie's attention was jerked away from Mrs. Fickling at once. Annie Cooper's lips were twisted with senseless rage, the kind of rage born from a dark place inside that had been created by endless hardship and suffering. She was raising the bowl again, crying, "You little thief! You scoundrel!"

"No!" Sarah screamed, wrapping her arms around Daphne in a desperate bid to protect her.

Mrs. Gantry, Mrs. Fickling, the servers who were still standing at the long tables – they were all watching without interest, as they always did when the girls fought. No one was going to stop Annie Cooper, no one except Doxie.

No matter what it cost.

She ran forward, covering the ground in long strides. With one arm – a strength rising in her born of sheer terror – she swept Daphne and Sarah out of the way. Her free hand seized Annie's arm and thrust the younger girl to the ground, knocking her backwards.

"Leave them alone!" she roared, pushing Daphne and Sarah to safety and standing over Annie with her hands on her hips. "Leave them alone! Never touch them again. Never bother them again! Ever! Do you understand me?"

Annie was staring up at her with round eyes, unhurt but terrified. Yet there was no time to feel any form of victory or relief. Mrs. Fickling's voice was the one that rang with triumph.

"You violent monster!" she cried. "Seize her, Mrs. Gantry! Seize her!"

There was no time to run, and even if there had been, Doxie had nowhere to run to. Mrs. Gantry bore down upon her like a charging bull. Seizing Doxie by the front of her dress, she lifted her terrifyingly off the ground, hanging helplessly by the threadbare garment. Spluttering and gasping, Doxie grabbed Mrs. Gantry's wrists and stared up at her in a mute plea. She could hear the dress ripping, feel violence trembling through Mrs. Gantry's clenched fists, see it burning in her eyes.

"Now you've done it," Mrs. Gantry hissed, relishing each triumphant syllable.

Mrs. Fickling strode nearer, her eyes gleaming with savage enjoyment. "You reckless, foolish girl," she spat. "How dare you strike one of the younger children? You bully!"

"Please," Doxie gasped, clinging to Mrs. Gantry's wrists. "Let me go."

"Oh, we're going to let you go," snarled Mrs. Fickling. She folded her arms. "I've had enough of you and of your insubordination."

Doxie felt her veins turn to ice. Half choking, tears streaming down her cheeks, she stared at Mrs. Fickling, shaking uncontrollably.

"Mrs. Gantry." Mrs. Fickling turned to the big woman, her eyes shining with malice. "Miss Shaw has been nothing but a menace ever since she arrived at this workhouse. For eight years I've put up with this bad, disobedient girl, and I've had just about enough."

"I couldn't agree more, ma'am," said Mrs. Gantry with considerable glee.

"Take her away." Mrs. Fickling waved a dismissive hand. "I never want to see her again. Send her out onto the streets – if she can't appreciate the charity that's been shown to her, then she is undeserving of it!"

Mrs. Gantry let go abruptly of Doxie's dress. She fell to the ground, gasping and clutching at the place where her dress had rubbed painfully on her throat. Before she could get her breath, Mrs. Gantry grabbed her arm, yanking her painfully to her feet.

"No! Doxie!" Sarah wailed.

"Hush, Sarah!" Doxie felt a thrill of fear run through her. She couldn't let Daphne and Sarah get into trouble. "Be a good girl. Be quiet!" She was crying as Mrs. Gantry dragged her toward the door. "Please, just be a good girl!"

She struggled to look back; Mrs. Gantry was pulling her so hard. But she managed a glance back at last, and saw Daphne and Sarah for the last time, clinging to one another, mute out of absolute terror. Their voices were silenced, but their eyes said it all.

Doxie had been their last hope, just as they had been hers.

EVEN AFTER THE workhouse door had been slammed shut behind Mrs. Gantry, Doxie stood in front of it for a few long, shocked moments, staring mutely at the building that had been her home for so long. At least, she supposed it had been her home. She had never thought of it that way, and there was certainly nothing sweet about it.

Perhaps it had never really been home, not the way home sounded in that old song, but it had still been the place where Doxie could have a roof over her head and food on the table. Now that she'd been thrown out, Doxie had no guarantee of where she could sleep tonight or when she would ever eat again.

She thought of the terrifying night she'd spent sleeping underneath Mr. Wainwright's produce stall, and her stomach clenched with fear. What was she going to do? Where could she go? She was too old to beg. She knew, also, that to be cast from one workhouse for breaking the rules was to be denied access to any of the others in London. She'd tried stealing, and it had ended in eight years in this terrible place, this place that had scarred and frightened her – but at least it had kept her alive. It was all she had known for so long, apart from the places where she'd been hired out.

The memory jolted something in her, made her straighten up and blink in the summer sun as if she was only now noticing it for the first time. She was, perhaps, doomed to spend her nights on the streets, to face the oncoming winter alone, to starve. But at least now she was free to do the one thing that she had been longing to do for four years.

She could finally return to Wylie Manor.

CHAPTER 15

EVEN THOUGH DOXIE'S body ached from being so roughly pulled around by Mrs. Gantry, and her stomach burned with hunger since one of the older women had stolen her breakfast, and she was facing a fate more uncertain than ever, she still found herself walking down the street with a spring in her step.

She knew that she must look entirely out of place walking among these manor houses in her faded workhouse clothing. The off-white dress, with its faded black stripes, was designed to stand out, to mark her as one who had been unable to cope in ordinary society like everyone else. In fact, Doxie was fairly sure that she could be arrested for stealing her workhouse clothes. Normally, Mrs. Fickling forced wayward inmates being banished from the workhouse to don whatever sorry rags they'd been wearing when they were admitted. In her triumph and fury, she must have forgotten.

Still, despite her hunger and her ugly clothes, Doxie felt excitement rising in her as she drew closer and closer to the last place where she'd been even remotely happy. Just around the next turn, Wylie Manor was waiting for her; she had made sure to memorize the way there so that she would always be able to find Owen. In just a few moments, she would be looking into his eyes again.

The last time Doxie had seen Owen, the sight of him had inspired something in her – a flutter deep in her belly, a flickering in the very pit of her soul. She realised now that in the past four years, though she hadn't seen him since she was just a little girl, the feeling had grown. It was rising now, from a spark to a flame to a bonfire, roaring in her soul and banishing all the other emotions that pressed her.

She could hardly breathe with the size and the heat of it as she reached the gate of the manor. It was even more beautiful now in the height of summer, and little had changed in the four years since Doxie had last been there. There was a wistaria climbing the front walls now, its blossoms brilliant against the old stone. The lawns were neatly mowed and beautifully green; the old orchard had grown, and its boughs hung low with golden pears and ripening apples.

Doxie was holding her breath as she followed the path between the lawns toward the servants' entrance. Instead of continuing up to the kitchens, however, she turned into the stable yard. It was a small yard, with a block of stables shaped like a horseshoe; as soon as Doxie stepped into it, she spotted the little Wylie girls' chestnut pony standing in the first stall. His little ears were pricked as he watched her coming into the yard.

Two of the stable doors were open, and she could hear the sound of a pitchfork scraping on stone coming from the nearest. Owen must be in there. Clasping her hands together, Doxie hesitated in front of the stable for a few unbearable moments. He had remembered her after their last long absence, and he had cared for her. Would it be the same now? Had he forgotten?

It was enough that she nearly turned and fled, but then a wheelbarrow rumbled within the stable, and she knew he was coming out into the yard. Her heart thundering, she waited, a smile growing on her face, as the wheelbarrow emerged from the stall... and it wasn't him.

The boy pushing the wheelbarrow was far younger than Owen; perhaps fourteen or fifteen. Owen must be nearly twenty years old now. Doxie stared at him in disappointment, and he returned her gaze with a glare of shock before speaking.

"What d'you want 'ere?" he said. "We don't need your kind begging on our grounds."

Doxie swallowed hard, glancing down at her workhouse stripes.

"I'm not here to beg, please," she said. "I... I'm just looking for Owen. Owen Green."

"Owen Green." The boy's eyes narrowed. "The previous stable boy."

Her heart thumped painfully. "Previous?" she stammered out.

"He's left." The boy started shoving the wheelbarrow across the yard.

"Left?" Doxie felt panic rising up in her, quenching the fire that had been blazing in her chest. "What do you mean – left?"

"I mean he's not 'ere anymore," snapped the boy. "Now, if you don't mind, I'm not some vagabond. I have work to do."

He marched out of the yard, leaving Doxie standing in the tatters of her hopes and dreams. It felt as though the world was spinning around her. She had never thought that she might someday get to Wylie Manor only for Owen to be somewhere else. She'd imagined him staying here, waiting for her, but he was gone.

Had he really forgotten her? If that was true, it meant that there was no one left in the world who cared about her.

Almost no one. She reached into her pocket, wrapping her trembling fingers around the spoon as she stood shaking in the stable yard, tears running down her cheeks. Someone, once, had loved her. They had loved her enough to leave a token with her, a tiny memento to help her remember that she had meant something. Perhaps she could mean something again someday.

But for now, she had to find a way to survive.

A loud voice floated down toward the stables from the direction of the kitchens. Doxie looked up, wiping at the tears on her cheeks. She knew that voice: it was Mrs. Cromwell, one of the few people who had ever been even remotely kind to Doxie. The cook was the only person Doxie could think of who might still help her.

Trudging up the path to the servants' entrance, Doxie tried to wipe away her tears and look cheerful. Mrs. Cromwell hated complaining, and she was determined to make a good impression. Reaching the door, she knocked once and stood back with her heart in her mouth.

It swung open, revealing a little girl in a maid's uniform. She stared up at Doxie, confused.

"Please," said Doxie, "I need to speak with Mrs. Cromwell."

"Who is it, Carrie?" Mrs. Cromwell's familiar voice called from inside the kitchen.

"I don't know," the little girl returned. "She's wearing workhouse clothes."

"Send her away! I don't have time for escapees," snorted Mrs. Cromwell.

"Mrs. Cromwell, please!" Doxie grabbed the door, stopping the little girl from slamming it shut. "Oh, please – it's me, Doxie. Doxie Shaw."

"Doxie?" Mrs. Cromwell came hurrying to the door, her arms held out, delight on her round face. "Oh, it really is you!" She grasped Doxie by the arms, staring up into her eyes. "How you've grown! Why, I thought perhaps you was dead."

"Why?" said Doxie, surprised by Mrs. Cromwell's warm welcome.

"Well, no one would ever tell me why the workhouse ignored my request," said Mrs. Cromwell. "They sent me some other little girl instead of you for the New Year's party all those years ago, and I specifically asked for you. It's the last time I made use of that workhouse, I can promise you that."

"The matron did it out of spite," said Doxie. "She knew I wanted to come back here, and she didn't let me, because I liked it here."

"The old hag!" said Mrs. Cromwell emphatically. Her eyes wandered over Doxie's striped dress. "Have you discharged yourself, then?"

"No, ma'am," said Doxie. "I... I was thrown out. She always did hate me." She took deep breaths, fighting to hold back her emotion. "Please, Mrs. Cromwell, do you know where Owen Green is?"

"Who's that?" asked Mrs. Cromwell.

"The stable boy... he was a friend."

"I'm afraid I don't know a thing about what's going on in those stables, dear," said Mrs. Cromwell.

Doxie felt as though her tattered heart was being kicked. She stared down at the floor, numb and speechless.

"I'm sorry, dear," said Mrs. Cromwell. "I have to get back to work."

Doxie looked up. "Work," she stammered. "I... I need work. Please, Mrs. Cromwell, do you have a position for me?"

Mrs. Cromwell cast a regretful glance into the kitchen, where the small girl was scrubbing the floor. "I'm sorry, Doxie," she said. "They appointed the little one just a few weeks ago. I don't have any work for you."

Doxie nodded, blinking back her tears, and Mrs. Cromwell reached out and put a hand on her arm. "But I think I know someone who might," she said. "Apple Grove – the manor house just down the street – lost a girl to consumption just last week. They're going to be needing another scullery-maid. Stand here for a moment, and I'll write you a recommendation."

"Oh, Mrs. Cromwell, thank you," Doxie gasped.

The cook bustled off, returning a few moments later with a folded note. She pressed it into Doxie's hand, folding her fingers around it. "There you are, child," she said, her voice warm and deep. "Take it and go to Apple Grove. They'll take you in, I'm sure of it." She sighed, biting her lip. "The cook there, Mrs. Howe, is a sharp-tongued woman. She'll be hard on you. I'm sorry. And the Roberts are a strange family. But work is better than nothing."

"Far better," agreed Doxie, managing a smile. "Thank you again, Mrs…"

But before she could finish expressing her gratitude, the door slammed. Mrs. Cromwell had gone back to work.

CHAPTER 16

FROM THE MOMENT Doxie had walked up the narrow servants' path to the back of Apple Grove, she'd known that this was nothing like Wylie Manor. There was no climbing wisteria here, no gnarled old orchard or cosy stable block. Everything here was set out in sharp, straight lines: square hedges bordering the rectangular lawns instead of flowerbeds, the corners of the house sharply geometric, the windows as tall and thin as those of the workhouse.

Even the kitchen and scullery lacked the cosiness of Wylie Manor. Doxie stood in it with her hands clasped behind her back, frankly astonished at how unbelievably clean this kitchen was. It was well-equipped, yet every ladle and spatula and rolling pin hung perfectly on the wall. The enormous tin sinks were gleaming like mirrors; the cupboard doors were all closed, there was no rug on the hearth, and the geometric grate was polished to a high shine.

The cleanliness of it all intimidated Doxie a little, and so did the woman who stood in front of the fire, frowning down at the letter that Mrs. Cromwell had written. She contrasted sharply with the kitchen. There was nothing spare about her strong jowls or stout figure, and pearls jingled around her neck as she moved; her spectacles hung on a silver chain.

She finally seemed to have perused the letter to her satisfaction, and she lowered it, looking up at Doxie.

"You're from the workhouse," she said flatly.

"Yes, ma'am," said Doxie, trembling a little and unsure of what she could say to sway this woman's opinion in her favour. "That's how I know Mrs. Cromwell. She hired me from the workhouse," she offered.

"That's what the letter says," said the cook acidly.

Doxie shut her mouth, deciding that silence may be her only chance at survival.

"Doxie," muttered the cook. "What kind of a first name is that?"

"I was an orphan, ma'am," said Doxie. "That's what the matron of the orphanage named me when she found me as a baby."

The cook glared at her for a few more moments, then sighed.

"Mrs. Cromwell doesn't take recommendations lightly," she said. "She recommended the last girl to me, too. She was a good little worker until consumption took her. Will you work hard too, Miss Shaw?"

"Yes, ma'am," said Doxie.

"Very well. Good help is hard to find; I'll accept you on trial, but you had better prove yourself, or you'll be out on your ear in no time," said the cook. "Do you understand?"

"Yes, ma'am," said Doxie.

"Good. You'd best get to work, then. You'll have twenty pounds a year, less your board, and a small sugar allowance, and we'll have to do something about a uniform to replace that ghastly dress. Your work begins at five in the morning and finishes when all is done – at nine or ten." The cook folded her arms, as if daring Doxie to protest.

She didn't know how much twenty pounds a year would come to each month, but it sounded like more money than she'd ever even heard of. "Yes, ma'am," she breathed. "Thank you, ma'am."

"Thank me once you've proven yourself," snapped the cook. "Until then, you're nothing to me. My name is Mrs. Howe, and you will address me only as such. Now, the parlour maids will be bringing the lunch dishes in at any moment. You are to wash them – and you will leave neither a chip nor the tiniest of stains on anything, do you understand?"

"Yes, ma'am," said Doxie, for what felt like the hundredth time.

Mrs. Howe snorted and then, having said her piece, swept out of the room. Doxie walked over to the sink, feeling almost too dirty even to touch it. She opened the tap and rinsed her hands first, then began to fill both sinks with water.

The simple motion of filling the sink made her breathing slow down a little. She felt herself beginning to let go of her fear, but it still sat in her stomach like she'd swallowed a hard, cold stone. She couldn't believe that Owen was gone. Where could he be? Would she ever see him again?

For so many years, he had been her only hope. She didn't know what she could cling to now, and if her hands hadn't been covered with soapy suds as she prepared the water for washing dishes, she would have reached into her pocket to feel for the spoon that still rested there. It was a mercy that Mrs. Fickling hadn't thought to force Doxie to give up her workhouse dress. She would have had to strip in front of the matron again, and this time she doubted the spoon would have escaped her notice. Doxie shuddered at the thought of what Mrs. Fickling would have done to her if she'd discovered that spoon.

The scullery doors banged open, and Doxie jumped, frightened. But instead of the intimidating Mrs. Howe, there were two girls coming into the room, each carrying a tray of dirty china and silver.

"Hello," Doxie said, smiling brightly at them.

The first girl simply gave Doxie a shocked look before putting the tray down on the spotless scullery table. The other, a jolly and round-faced person with beautifully curly black hair, gave Doxie a little grimace. Glancing around the scullery as she set down her tray, she turned to Doxie, speaking in a whisper.

"Hello!" she hissed. "Mrs. Howe doesn't allow talking while we work, but I'm glad to meet you."

Doxie liked her instantly. "Glad to meet you, too," she whispered.

"Hey!" boomed an angry voice from the adjacent kitchen. "Are you girls talking in there?"

"No, ma'am!" said the curly-haired girl brightly. She gave Doxie a wink, then disappeared off into the kitchen along with the other parlour maid.

Doxie picked up a stack of glasses. They were mostly bronze, she noticed, and rather old-fashioned, but at least they were less stressful to wash than glass. Sinking them deep into the soapy water, she picked one out and began to scrub it.

It was only when she had washed one side and turned it over to get started on the other that she noticed the emblem.

Doxie's heart stood still. She stared at it, gently wiping the suds away, almost unable to believe what her eyes were seeing. It was there, more intricate than she'd ever seen it before, but clear as day: a delicate engraving of a simple flower, its five petals as sharp as the points of a star.

Her heart was thundering in her throat. She glanced around the scullery, but she was alone. Reaching into her pocket, she drew out the spoon and held it up against the glass.

The similarity was unmistakable. Even though the engraving on the spoon's handle had been worn almost smooth by Doxie's touch over the years, she could see it, clear as day.

The emblem on the bronze glass exactly matched the one on the handle of Doxie's silver spoon.

CHAPTER 17

THE UNIFORM that Mrs. Howe had ordered made for Doxie was the first piece of clothing she had ever worn that actually fit her – and it fit perfectly.

There were many things about working at Apple Grove that she didn't love, but that uniform was something she adored. Stepping back on the box she was using to reach the back window of the scullery, Doxie took a moment to look at her reflection. The last time she'd really looked in a mirror had been when she was a little girl in the orphanage. She wasn't sure when her body had changed so much, curves appearing where there had once been only angular lines, but she liked the way that the black dress flowed over it.

It was a small thing, but Doxie had to hold onto whatever small things could still bring her a little joy. Stepping forward again, she went on scrubbing the window with a piece of old newspaper, rubbing away dust and pollen. Thinking about her new dress helped her not to think about Owen, about how she'd gone down to the stables and asked everyone she saw whether they knew him, only to be chased off in scorn by the angry stablemaster who didn't want her "flirting" with the stable lads. She wasn't interested in anyone in that way.

Anyone except, perhaps, Owen; but she would only know if she saw him again and finding him felt impossible. Even if she did find him, what could she say? Would he even remember her? Would they still be friends?

Could they be more?

She dragged her thoughts away from Owen and went on trying to untangle the mystery of the emblem on her spoon. She'd seen it all over the house: on the china, on the glasses, on the many other silver teaspoons she washed every single day. It felt so strange to see replicas of the spoon she so cherished; less tarnished, less worn, but nonetheless the same. She ached to know where her spoon had come from.

Perhaps one of the women she worked with was her mother…

There was movement in the reflection on the window. Doxie glanced over her shoulder. A carriage was coming up the drive, which ran parallel to the servants' path for some distance. The sharp-pointed flower was painted on the doors of the carriage, too; Doxie assumed that it was an apple blossom.

She watched the horses go by, vaguely curious about the family whose dishes she washed; she'd never yet seen their faces. They drove around toward the stable yard, and then she heard a female voice calling out from inside the carriage. It came to an abrupt halt, and the doors opened. An elderly couple and two ladies, in their thirties or so, stepped out.

The elderly lady had stopped to point out something in the long row of roses growing alongside the hedge, and she didn't look pleased about it. She called the gardener over, and the poor man stood with his head bowed as she began to give him what sounded like a thorough tongue-lashing.

Doxie felt bad for the gardener, but worse for the two young ladies. They were standing behind their mother, their heads hanging, their cheeks reddening.

"Yep, that's the family of the house," said a cheery voice below Doxie.

She looked down. The curly-haired maid, whose name was Agnes, was busy taking out the garbage. With Mrs. Howe busy at the stove, it was one of the rare occasions during working hours when they could talk without the risk of being beaten or locked in a cupboard as punishment.

"The young ladies seem so unhappy," said Doxie.

"Mr. and Mrs. Roberts are two stiff old birds. I wouldn't like to be the daughters," said Agnes. "I'm sure Mr. Roberts eats every suitor alive. That's why they're both old maids, you know. The eldest one, Celeste, she's thirty-four already, and no man will touch her. Old Mr. Roberts frightens them all away."

"Mrs. Roberts seems a little sharp too," said Doxie.

"Why do you think she appointed Mrs. Howe as her housekeeper?" Agnes gave a cynical laugh.

Mrs. Roberts appeared to have finished her tongue-lashing. The gardener drooped off miserably, and she swept back into the carriage, closely followed by Mr. Roberts. The girls trailed along in their wake. The older one, the one that Agnes called Celeste, had a defeated look to the slump of her shoulders that made Doxie feel a little sad for her.

"You're right," she said. "I do feel sorry for them."

"Silly, ain't it?" Agnes grinned up at her. "They've got all the food they can ever eat, and they'll never have to do a stitch of work in their lives."

"I suppose," said Doxie.

She knew that it was true, and that the Roberts girls had everything they could ever want. Still, Doxie couldn't help feeling pity for them, even though she was a poor scullery-maid in their employ.

THE ORPHAN'S SILVER SPOON

THE ONLY TIME that Doxie had off from work, apart from nights, was on a Sunday afternoon between one and five. As soon as the lunch dishes had been washed, the kitchen staff all had a brief break before preparations for tea would begin.

The first week or two, Doxie had spent her Sunday afternoon the same way as the other girls did: curled up on her bunk, catching up on some much-needed sleep. But something was eating at her, something almost as urgent as the questions she had about the emblem on her spoon that matched the Apple Grove emblem. The spark in her, the thing that longed so constantly for Owen, was growing and growing with every day that she didn't know his fate. Ultimately, she had to do something to find out.

Doxie walked up the pathway to Wylie Manor, trying to enjoy the warm sunshine on her face instead of worrying over what the master and mistress would say if they noticed that the same scullery-maid had come visiting their servants for the third week in a row.

It truly was a beautiful day. The sunshine shone down through the leaves of the orchard, dappling richly on the deep green grass, where geese floated like ships through the waving grass. Doxie took a deep breath, squaring her shoulders. Perhaps today would be the day that she finally found answers.

She walked into the stable yard just as the uncouth stable boy was walking out of it. His face had been washed, and there was a relatively clean red neck-kerchief peeping out from his shirt; his clean-scrubbed cheeks were rosy with excitement. But when his eyes landed on hers, they crinkled in an angry scowl.

"Not you again!" he said furiously. "I told you, I don't know nothing about no Owen Green, and the stablemaster won't talk to you either."

"Please," said Doxie. "If you could just ask him... I'll be here again this time next week." Her heart was sinking; despite the bright sunshine that was still pouring down upon her, she felt as though a dark cloud had descended over her day.

"He doesn't want to talk to you," snapped the boy. "None of us do. In fact, if you come here again, I'll tell the master that you're a thief and he'll set the dogs on you!"

She reached into her pocket, running her thumb back and forth over the emblem on her spoon. "I don't want to cause any trouble. I just want to know what happened to Owen Green."

"Well, I just want you to go away," spat the boy. "Go on! Be off with you!"

Doxie backed away, and the boy bent down, grasping a half-brick that was lying on the cobbles of the yard. "Go away!" he shouted, raising it threateningly.

Doxie had no choice. Tears filled her eyes, and she turned to run, her feet carrying her in stumbling strides away from the manor that was her only hope of ever finding Owen. The brick smashed to the ground just a few feet away from her, and she increased her speed, running back down the hill past the orchard where she'd seen him on that snowy day so many years ago.

She only stopped when she'd burst through the gate, and then stood weeping on the road, trying to control the tears that gushed down her cheeks. She knew the boy would make good on his threat – or perhaps just stone her himself for good measure. She could never return to Wylie Manor.

Taking deep, shaky breaths, Doxie realized she was still clutching her spoon in her hand. The street was quiet, so she opened her hand and looked down at it. It shone a little in the sun; the emblem almost worn smooth by her touch. But it was still the apple blossom emblem, the one she saw every day at Apple Grove, and it sent a jolt of hope running through her.

Doxie squared her shoulders. If she wasn't going to find Owen at Wylie Manor, she'd have to try looking at the stable yards of the other manor houses around here. He must be around here somewhere. She would find him somehow.

She would have to, or she feared her heart wouldn't survive the blow.

CHAPTER 18

Doxie couldn't believe how much food the Roberts family wasted every day. It seemed like the two young ladies ate like birds, if they ate at all; she could hardly imagine how they were still alive. If she had been given the meals with which they were presented three or even four times a day – with eggs and cake and bread and meat and fruit and vegetables, gravy and potatoes, and salads, piping hot roasts dripping with fat – then she knew she would never turn down any of it, not a scrap.

Yet now she was standing with one of the china plates in her hand, a whole slice of roast beef lying on the patterned surface, still swimming in congealed gravy against a mound of golden mashed potatoes. Why would they dish up the food only to stare at it? None of it made sense to Doxie, who'd had bread and butter for lunch, and whose stomach was growling in anticipation of a plain supper.

Still, she knew that to touch that food would be to invite endless vitriol from Mrs. Howe. Though it made her ache inside, she knocked the food into the dustbin, closing the lid quickly so that she wouldn't see it lying there.

"Makes no sense, does it?" said Agnes, who had just bustled into the kitchen with another tray of dirty dishes.

Doxie glanced around in panic. Agnes laughed. "Mrs. Howe's gone out," she said. "We're out of flour; she left in a flap. She can't hear us talking."

"Oh," said Doxie, relieved. She smiled at Agnes, glad of the friendly girl's company as she plunged the plate into the soapy water. "No, it doesn't make any sense at all. I don't understand why those ladies turn down such good food."

"Rich folk." Agnes shrugged. "They're funny things." She paused, thinking about it. "Maybe you'd be put off your supper, too, if you had Mrs. Roberts for a mother."

Doxie laughed. "Agnes! You can't say that."

"Seems I just did." Agnes gave her a wicked grin. "But don't you think it's true?"

"I wouldn't know; I don't know what it's like to have a mother." Doxie lifted the plate out of the water and gave it a last scrub. And there it was again, that emblem, the sharp-edged apple blossom, the one that held so many answers.

"You don't?" said Agnes, looking up at Doxie in surprise.

"No," Doxie murmured, gazing at the emblem. "I... I never knew my mother."

It was true, but in a way, she felt she had always known her mother. Ever since the day that Miss Claire had placed that spoon in her hand, she had known something about her, had felt her love and presence every time she touched its smooth surface.

And now perhaps she was standing in the very same kitchen where her mother – where someone she could have called *Mama* – had once worked. Where perhaps Mama still worked, although Doxie doubted it; none of the women here seemed to bear much resemblance to her. Would she know her mother if she looked into her eyes?

"Doxie?" Agnes waved a hand in front of her face. "You've wandered off a bit, love."

"Oh – sorry." Doxie startled a little, realising that she was still staring down at the plate and the emblem. She lowered it into the rinse water.

"Is everything all right with you?" asked Agnes. "You've been acting strange ever since you came back on Sunday afternoon."

Doxie made an attempt at a smile. She knew she was acting strange; she was feeling strange, as though a great boulder had been strapped to her chest. She had lost her last chance to find Owen, and the knowledge left her rudderless and adrift on a vast and lonely sea.

"I... I've been trying to find someone," said Doxie. "Someone I care about very much but haven't seen in a very long time."

Agnes' eyes filled with empathy. "Oh, I'm sorry," she said. "Who is it?"

Doxie set the plate on the draining board and realised that she didn't know if she was talking about Owen or her mother. She looked up at Agnes, a yearning rising up in her, one that she had been fighting hard to suppress; a yearning to ask, to find out about her mother, about the spoon. But she knew that if she showed the wrong person the spoon, they would assume that either Doxie or her mother had stolen it. And wasn't that the most likely explanation? The one thing that Doxie knew for sure about her mother was that she'd been a thief.

"A... a boy," she stammered out, her heart breaking.

"Oh!" Agnes giggled with glee. "Tell me everything."

Doxie forced a smile. She wanted to find Owen more than almost anything, but not quite anything.

Finding out who her mother had been, that was her heart's greatest desire.

Doxie's feet were tired as she trudged down the street, bordered with the green lawns and tree-lined driveways of manor houses. She wasn't the only girl in a maid's uniform walking the streets at this hour; most of the houses around here allowed their maids a few hours off around this time. In fact, the streets were quite busy with servants. Old housekeepers strolled along quietly, enjoying a little of the summer sun. Stable boys played marbles on the streets, cursing fluidly. Gnarled old gardeners sat on benches in the tiny park nearby, gazing at nothing. Girls giggled past, hanging on the arms of dashing young men. None of them were Owen. Doxie wondered if he had grown dashing by now; perhaps he always had been, but she hadn't been old enough to know it yet.

At any rate, he wasn't on this street, and he hadn't been at any of the stable yards where she'd searched for him. All afternoon, she'd been going from one manor to the other, asking one stablemaster after the other if he knew of Owen Green. Many of them chased her from the yard before she could even ask; others were helpful but didn't know him.

It was as if he had disappeared completely from the face of the earth.

Doxie took a deep breath, trying to dispel the utter terror that clutched at her heart at the thought that Owen might be... *No.* She couldn't allow herself to think that. If Owen was truly gone, and she couldn't ask about her mother, then she had nothing; nothing in all the world. She was teetering on the brink of losing hope already. She had to keep herself from going over the edge.

Reaching the crossroads, Doxie hovered for a moment, irresolute. One road led around the block back to Apple Grove and home. The other, down the street that passed Wylie Manor. She didn't know if she had the strength to walk past that place again, knowing that Owen wouldn't be standing in the orchard, waving to her...

The church bell chimed, and Doxie sighed. She only had half an hour left before she needed to be back at Apple Grove, and her limbs were exhausted. Weary heart and weary legs collided, and the weary legs won. She turned down the street that passed Wylie Manor and started stumbling down the familiar road.

As soon as the gentle lines of Wylie Manor came into view, Doxie regretted it. It felt as though her heart would burst with pressure, with the unrelenting build-up of love that so sorely lacked its subject, and Doxie hung her head, keeping her eyes trained on the paving so she wouldn't look up at the last place where she'd been even remotely happy. She reached into her pocket, traced her thumb over the emblem on her spoon. Even that felt tainted these days. It was so close to giving her answers, yet to ask for those answers would be to risk her very livelihood.

"Hi! Hello! Miss!"

Doxie ducked her head, walking a little faster. The masculine voice that called after her was loud and rough, and she didn't want any trouble. She couldn't afford any trouble.

"Miss! Miss!" it bellowed. There were running feet on the earth behind her. "Hey! Stop!"

Doxie's heart leapt into her mouth, thundering like a runaway horse. She broke into a jog, glancing over her shoulder; there was a man on the other side of the palisade fence, running across the lawn of Wylie Manor, his eyes fixed on her. She didn't know him, but he was looking right at her.

"Miss! Stop!" he yelled. "Stop! I won't hurt you! I just want to tell you about Owen Green!"

The name brought Doxie to a stumbling halt. Shock rippled through her body, combining with the fear that thrilled in her every cell; yet she would have gladly faced a minotaur or a fire-breathing chimera if it could lead her to Owen.

She turned slowly, her heart fluttering in her chest like a wild bird, and the man who jogged to a halt on the other side of the palisades was neither a minotaur nor a chimera. In fact, now that she no longer looked upon him with eyes clouded by fear, he was an ugly but ordinary human being. His nose was crooked, his teeth were yellow, and only a few tufts of greying hair clung to his mottled and liver-spotted crown; but the warm brown eyes that twinkled out at her from deep within their sockets held a warm kindness more splendid than any head of golden hair.

"Are you the girl?" he asked. "The one who worked at Wylie Manor, who keeps asking about Owen?"

"Yes," Doxie breathed. "I'm his friend... Doxie Shaw."

"Doxie Shaw. That's right." The man smiled, a happy creasing of his entire face. "Owen nearly stayed on as stable boy because of you. He wanted to make sure that you would always be able to find him."

"He... he did?" Doxie breathed.

"He did." The man chuckled. "He's a good lad, Owen. Kind-hearted. Hard-working. And loyal to a fault, as you can see. I'm the one who convinced him to go."

"Go where?" asked Doxie.

"Why, he's a stablemaster himself now," said the man. "He worked as stable lad under me. Now he runs a stable, and he's already better than I ever was."

"Where?" Doxie gasped.

"Laurel Hall. He begged me to tell you, if you ever came, where he had gone. Of course, young Alfred couldn't be bothered. I apologise for his insolence," said the stablemaster. "He's doing very well for himself, young miss. In fact, if you come by here after work, I'll take you to Laurel Hall myself. It's not a long walk, but I fear you'll lose your way."

"Oh, sir!" Tears of joy began to gush down Doxie's cheeks. "Oh, please, please, sir!"

"Now, now, none of that," said the stablemaster curtly. "Run along now. Get back to your work – I see you're dressed as a maid – and then come over here when you're done, and I'll take you to him. Dry your eyes, miss. There's no need for that noise."

"Thank you," Doxie croaked, wiping frantically at her cheeks. "Thank you."

"Run along," said the man gruffly. "I'll see you tonight."

He turned and strode away, and Doxie went on to Apple Grove feeling as though the very air itself had suddenly turned brightly golden with joy.

CHAPTER 19

THE WALK to Laurel Hall was beautiful, even though it was very late that evening that Doxie met up with Mr. Thornton, the stablemaster of Wylie Manor. She had worked hard that evening, yet her entire body had been buzzing with excitement the moment she saw him waiting at Wylie Manor's gate. He said very little to her, seeming uncomfortable with the joy that was rushing through her in a golden tide, but they walked companionably together through the streets. Occasionally he would remark on a place where she needed to avoid the fence because of vicious dogs or a turn that was easily missed.

It was a perfect summer night. There was not a breath of wind, and the stars above were brilliantly bright. Streetlamps pooled golden light onto the neat paving. But it was all lost on Doxie; her eyes strained ahead, waiting to see Owen's dear face, waiting to hear from him at last if it was true what Mr.

Thornton had said, that he really had left a message for her, that he hadn't abandoned her after all.

Laurel Hall itself was just as beautiful. It was larger and grander than Wylie Manor, with white rose bushes bordering even the drive leading up to the stables, tinting the night with their extravagant fragrance. The stables were well-lit, a gas lamp above each door, and Doxie stood trembling in the yard as curious horses watched her, shining softly in their stables. Mr. Thornton had gone up to the loft rooms above the stables, and she heard him knocking on the door. Then a voice; the door was around the corner, and she could see nothing, and barely hear, but she knew it at once. It was Owen.

She feared her knees might buckle and she might crumple to the floor in a trembling heap of sheer delight. But when he came around the corner, walking quickly, his eyes alight, he had the opposite effect on her. Her limbs were set suddenly on fire. She rushed across the cobbles, her heart thundering in her throat, and stopped short just a few feet from him, her hands outstretched as though to wrap him in her arms.

She took in his dear face in one delighted glance. He had grown up a little; there was a stubble of beard on his jaw now, and the lines of his cheeks and temples held something sterner than in past years. But the blue eyes were the same. And when he smiled his crooked, gap-toothed smile, that was the same too, and it lit up everything within her. The spark that had burned so low became a roaring wildfire in her chest, capturing her breath, wrapping her heart in blazing warmth.

"Owen," she gasped.

"Oh, Doxie." He strode toward her then, and caught up her hands in his own, wrapping them in warm and strong and work-worn fingers. "I knew you'd come. I knew it."

"Of course, I came," said Doxie. "You're my dearest friend."

He closed his hands around hers a little tighter.

"You've always been my best friend," he whispered huskily.

With everything in her, Doxie loved those words; and also with everything in her, she wanted to be so much more.

※

DOXIE SIGHED with exhaustion as she walked into the tiny room where she slept. It was only Wednesday, yet already she was longing for those few precious hours of rest that were afforded her on a Sunday afternoon – and for far more than rest, too. Her lips lifted in a smile as she sat down on her narrow bed and started pulling her shoes from her aching feet. She couldn't wait to return to Laurel Hall that Sunday afternoon, and spend it picnicking with Owen, catching up on all the years they had missed. He had seemed as happy to see her as she'd been to see him.

"And what are you smiling about, then?" asked a cheerful voice.

Doxie looked up. Agnes was standing in the doorway, grinning impishly. Somehow, despite their long hours, her happy friendliness seemed unabated.

Doxie couldn't smother a rather girlish giggle.

"Oh!" Agnes' eyes widened. "You found him, then? The boy?"

"I did." Doxie let out a tiny squeal of delight. "Oh, Agnes, I really did!"

"Doxie!" Agnes rushed into the room and flopped companionably onto the bed beside her. "Tell me everything. Where is he? Who is he?"

"He's the stablemaster at Laurel Hall," said Doxie.

"A stablemaster!" Agnes gasped. "Why, Doxie, you're getting ideas above your station." Her sparkling eyes said she was teasing. "Is he very old?"

"No, no! He's only nineteen or twenty," said Doxie.

"Well, that's wonderful," said Agnes. "I'm glad you found him."

"So am I." Doxie smiled, but a note of sadness rose in her heart. She reached into her pocket, touching the spoon. There was something left that she had to find somehow. Looking up at Agnes, her friendly smile, her dancing eyes, she wondered if there could really be in any danger in asking her about her mother. Agnes would never betray her.

"Agnes, can I ask you something?" she asked.

"Of course," said Agnes. She folded her arms. "I've had many beaus. I can give you good advice."

"Not about that." Doxie laughed, then paused. "Do you... do you know if anyone ever stole a spoon from the kitchen?"

"Stole?" Agnes shuddered. "Why, Doxie, I can't imagine that anyone would dare. Imagine what Mrs. Howe would do to them!"

Doxie thought she could imagine.

"Why do you ask?" Agnes gave her a worried look. "You're not..."

"No." Doxie shook her head. "I would never steal, Agnes. You know that."

"Oh. I suppose I do." Agnes' face relaxed into her usual happy smile. "So, why do you ask?"

"I... uh..." Doxie had to think fast. She couldn't tell Agnes the truth; not if she had already been suspicious of Doxie just a few seconds ago. "I thought there might be a spoon missing tonight while I was washing the dishes," she said at last. "I found it in the end, but I was worried someone had stolen it."

"Well, I don't know," said Agnes. "I suppose someone must have, at some point. But not that I know of. Still, it's probably best you keep an eye on the number of spoons, Doxie. A lot of people have sticky fingers – and they have a way of making everything much harder for those of us who are honest."

Doxie nodded enthusiastically to show her agreement, but inside, her heart was sinking. Not only did Agnes not know Doxie's mother, but she'd also proven that Doxie's fears were true: asking these kind of questions could only get her in trouble.

She'd have to decide if finding out her mother's name would be worth that trouble.

CHAPTER 20

Summer was marching slowly to its close, and it was as though the twilight of the season's life was the most glorious of all its days. The sunlight seemed all the richer and more golden for the way it filtered through leaves that were now tinged with yellow along the edges; the sky much bluer for the fluffy grey clouds that sculled peacefully across its surface.

In fact, even though Doxie's feet ached with exhaustion and she'd just eaten her first real square meal in weeks, she might have considered herself the happiest she'd ever been as she lay stretched out on the blue-and-white picnic blanket spread out beneath the sheltering boughs of the old oak tree in the home paddock. There was a little brook running down the bottom of the small paddock, and the grass was cropped close and perfectly green. A few horses grazed along the banks of the stream; their summer coats brilliant in the sun.

No part of the scenery, however, could match the beauty of Owen's eyes. He lay propped on one elbow on the other side of the picnic blanket, the basket acting as chaperone in between them, but his blue eyes caressed her face in a way that made goosebumps rise on her skin.

"Can you believe summer is nearly over?" he said. "It feels like it was only yesterday that you walked into the stable yard at last, yet nearly three months have passed."

"I know." Doxie smiled. "But at the same time, it feels like we've been meeting on Sunday afternoons for an entire lifetime."

Owen laughed in a way that filled her belly with golden bubbles. "I know what you mean," he said. "I don't know how I ever lived without you, Doxie."

Those words made her feel warm inside, and she returned his smile with all of her heart. "Neither do I," she whispered.

Owen watched her for a few long moments. "Have you eaten enough?" he asked.

"Yes, thank you." Doxie grinned. The picnic had been a plain affair – bread and butter, apples and cheese – but it had been ample. Far more so than the fare afforded to the servants at Apple Grove, in any case. Doxie looked forward to Sunday afternoons mostly because of Owen, but truth be told, she was always excited for the meal as well. It was the one day in her week in which she went to bed with a truly full stomach.

A pained look came into Owen's eyes. "I wish you'd let me send some home with you," he said. "I earn enough, you know, to give you all the bread you need."

"I know you do." Doxie smiled, hoping to put his mind at ease. "It's not about that. I just don't want any trouble with Mrs. Howe or the girls."

"I know." Owen sighed. "I'm still trying to get you appointed here, at Laurel Hall. They're kin of the Wylies and they'd take far better care of you, just as they have taken better care of me."

"I'm sure they would," said Doxie, without enthusiasm.

Owen gave her a surprised glance. "You don't sound as though you'd be interested in working here," he said.

"I'd love to work here." Doxie smiled at him. "I'd love to see you every single day. But..." She paused, wondering how to put it into words. "Owen, I'm so close to finding out more about my mother. About where I come from. I... I can't walk away from Apple Grove now."

Owen shook his head. "I know this is important to you," he said. "I just wish you wouldn't keep trying to find things out. What if your mother really did steal that spoon, Doxie? Maybe they'll be angry with you. Maybe she did worse than steal the spoon, too. And apart from that, those are dangerous questions to be asking. You could get yourself dismissed. You could get yourself beaten." His voice lowered, trembling with fear. "You could get yourself arrested."

"I won't." Doxie smiled at him, reaching over the picnic blanket to wrap her hand around his strong, calloused fingers. "I'm being careful. That's why I haven't found anything out in months."

"Please, Doxie." Owen gave a shaky sigh. "Keep being careful. I know how much this means to you." He lowered his eyes, a redness creeping over his cheeks. "But you don't know how much you mean to me."

OWEN'S WORDS had been weighing on Doxie's mind all week, and they weighed on her still as she swept the scullery floor late that Saturday night.

She was almost alone in the kitchen. Only Hester, one of the kitchen-maids, was still up; she was kneeling by the kitchen grate, stoking the fire that crackled there one last time to warm the kitchen and the servants' quarters through the night. Despite being a maid, Hester was an older woman, old enough to be Doxie's mother. But there was nothing of Hester in Doxie's face. Hester's hook nose, high cheekbones, and wispy grey-blonde hair was nothing like what Doxie saw when she looked in the mirror.

Still, Hester was the one person whom Doxie had not yet asked about her mother. And she was old enough that perhaps she'd remember a pregnant girl working in these kitchens, fleeing in the night, taking one of their silver spoons with her.

Turning away to sweep the back corner of the scullery, working toward the door into the kitchen, Doxie paused to slip a hand into her pocket and run her fingers over the reassuring surface of the spoon. Maybe Owen was right. Maybe this whole mystery was best left alone. Yet it had been niggling at her for so long, nagging and tugging at her heart and soul, that she couldn't stop. She had to find out where her mother had come from.

Working her way out into the kitchen, Doxie gave a last glance around to check for Mrs. Howe. Not seeing her, she spoke.

"Chilly this evening, isn't it?" she said.

Hester glanced up from the fire, her pinched face brutally painted in the yellow light. "No," she grunted.

The dour response was discouraging. Doxie bit her lip, continuing to sweep for a few more moments.

Then Hester seemed to relent. "Not yet, anyways," she said. "The real cold's still coming."

"Yes, you're right," said Doxie. "It's only just September, after all."

Hester grunted in response.

Doxie took a deep breath. She had to try. Hester was her last chance.

"You've been working here a while, haven't you, Hester?" she said.

Hester gave her a sidelong glance. "Thirty years this winter," she said. "I was a mite like you when I started."

Thirty years. Doxie's heart raced. Hester must have known her mother then; Doxie herself was just over seventeen.

"You've known a lot of people who worked in these kitchens over the years, then," she said casually.

"Many," murmured Hester. Her eyes grew contemplative. "Many."

Doxie swallowed hard. She stepped forward. "Anyone who looked like... like me?" she said.

Hester looked up at her, her eyes wide. "Now why would you ask such a thing?" she cried, leaping to her feet.

Doxie knew immediately that she'd crossed a line and tried frantically to uncross it. "I just... I..."

"Do tell, Miss Shaw." The voice came from behind her, turning her blood to ice. "Why *would* you ask such a thing?"

Doxie turned slowly, trembling. Mrs. Howe stood behind her in the doorway, her arms folded, the angles of her elbows as sharp in the firelight as the look in her eyes.

"F-foolishness, ma'am," was all that Doxie could croak out.

Mrs. Howe's eyes narrowed. She took a few steps forward. "I know foolishness when I see it," she snapped. "I still want to know why. The other girls have been complaining about your stupid questions for weeks. What are you getting at? What is it that you hope to find out?"

Doxie's mind was racing. Perhaps a version of the truth would satisfy this woman, would save Doxie from whatever dark fate Mrs. Howe was contemplating.

"I'm an orphan, ma'am," she said. "I know nothing about my mother. I'm always just trying to find something out about her or my family, that's all."

Mrs. Howe took another step forward, her nose mere inches from Doxie's, anger burning in her eyes.

"You're a liar," she hissed.

"No!" Doxie gasped. "No, please, ma'am, it's all true." She read danger in Mrs. Howe's face. "Please, I just want to find my mother. I just want to know where I come from."

"And why would you think that you would find answers here, at Apple Grove?" Mrs. Howe spat.

Doxie realized there were tears of terror flowing down her cheeks.

"I d-d-don't know," she sobbed.

"Well, child, then you'll never find out." Mrs. Howe stepped back, her mannerism changing abruptly. "If you'd told me the truth, perhaps I would have told you what I know. But you won't. So you'll never know, never in your life."

Mrs. Howe's words shattered something inside Doxie, something panicky and desperate. She rushed forward, grabbing at the cook's arm. "Please!" she cried. "Please - do you know who my mother is?"

"I won't tell you," snapped Mrs. Howe. "Not unless you tell me the truth - the full truth." Her eyes glittered coldly. "Why do you think that your mother had anything to do with this manor, Miss Shaw?"

Perhaps this was Doxie's one chance. Her only hope at ever finding out who her mother was. Heart hammering, she knew that she had to try. She couldn't let this final hope pass her by. Reckless with terror, she blurted the words.

"Because of the spoon," she whispered.

Darkness filled Mrs. Howe's eyes. "What spoon?" she snapped.

Doxie had never let anyone see that spoon, not since Miss Claire. Taking it from her pocket felt like undressing in public, like being stripped naked in that workhouse, but she would do anything - anything - to find out more about her mother.

"This one," she whispered.

Mrs. Howe's eyes widened. "Thief!" she shrieked, lunging forward. "Thief and liar!"

"No! No!" cried Doxie. "I didn't take it! They found it with me - at the orphanage!"

But Mrs. Howe was too quick. Her claws reached out, snatching the spoon from Doxie's very hand as she spoke. She skittered backward, clutching it.

"Thief!" she yelled again.

"No, no!" Terror filled Doxie's heart at the sight of her spoon in Mrs. Howe's hand. Her empty pocket made her feel anchorless, as though the wind might just blow it away, as though she'd never existed at all. "Give it back!"

She lunged forward. Mrs. Howe reached out a hand, slamming it painfully into Doxie's cheek. Stumbling back, she fell to the floor, panicked and sobbing.

"Go!" roared Mrs. Howe, her eyes burning, the spoon held high out of Doxie's reach, her only link to her past taken from her. "Get out of this manor. Be gone!"

"Please," Doxie sobbed, her voice breathy and frantic now, coming out in tiny gasps of terror. "Please, please, please, give it back."

"Go!" shrieked Mrs. Howe. "Go or I'll set the dogs on you!"

Doxie knew that those dogs would tear her limb from limb. She stumbled to her feet, tears still pouring down her cheeks. Yet even as she bolted from the kitchen, ran down the long geometric pathway and crashed out into the cold wind that blew down the street, she felt that even that mauling would be less painful than leaving the spoon behind.

CHAPTER 21

Doxie was exhausted with sobbing by the time she reached the blessed familiarity of the path leading up to the stables at Laurel Hall. As she stumbled into the yard, she felt as though her distraught presence was an intrusion on a world of ethereal peace. The horses were all dozing with their heads over the doors; some of them looked up as she came wandering in, but in the still, cool night, there was almost no sound.

Owen was on the far end of the yard, holding up a lantern as he peered into the stall of the old cob standing there. He was stroking its face, murmuring to it, and seemed locked in a world of his own. Doxie stood there for a few minutes, panting and sobbing, before he turned around and saw her.

The lantern wobbled in his grip; he almost dropped it. "Doxie!" he gasped, rushing to her. "What's happened? You've been crying. Are you hurt?"

"Oh, Owen, you were right." A fresh flood of tears overwhelmed Doxie. "I should have listened to you. I should have listened!"

She began to weep wholeheartedly, and Owen came over to her, reaching out to lay a strong hand on her shoulder. It gave her a tiny bit of strength, enough to sob out some more words.

"I should never have asked questions," she cried. "I should never have asked about my mother. Now I've lost the last little bit of her that I had left."

"Doxie, what happened?" asked Owen.

"Mrs. Howe took it." The words ripped Doxie open, tearing apart her aching heart. "She took my spoon, Owen."

"Oh, Doxie." Owen's voice was filled with empathy.

"After all these years," Doxie sobbed. "I kept it safe for all these years. And now it's gone... it's just gone. I don't know what to do." She reached into her pocket, but her hands found only empty air, and panic clutched at her. "I'm lost, Owen. I'm lost without it. I have nothing."

"You've lost something, but not everything, and not yourself." Owen's voice was deep and a little hurt. "Doxie, you still have me."

She raised her face to his, seeking strength in his serene blue eyes. "I just wanted to know her name," she whispered.

"I know. I know." He squeezed her shoulder, his tone gentle. "Do you... have somewhere to sleep tonight?"

Fresh fear gripped Doxie's chest. "No," she whispered. "I... I'm dismissed. I have nowhere to go. No work, no..."

"Hush." Owen smiled at her; his eyes filled with love. "Don't worry about that just now. You can't come up to my room with me, but there's space for you in the hay loft; it will be warm over old Plodder's stable. You'll be safe, my darling, and I'll bring you some supper. And we'll work out all of these things in the morning."

Doxie felt her shoulders slumping. "Thank you," she whispered. "You're so good to me."

Owen smiled at her. "Come," he said, taking her hand. "Everything will be all right."

Doxie trailed after him across the stable yard. She couldn't say it to him, not after everything he was doing for her, but she knew that everything was a long way from all right.

She couldn't go on without that spoon.

AND SO IT WAS, late that night when the last candle that Doxie could see flickering in Owen's window had been blown out, that she rose from her bed of fragrant hay, slipped down the ladder, jogged across the stable yard, and slipped off purposefully in the direction of Apple Grove.

CHAPTER 22

DOXIE FELT as though she was holding her heart in her mouth, where it trembled with fear as she stayed in the shadows of the tall hedges that lined the driveway at Apple Grove. The moon was far too bright; brilliantly silver, it poured down over the lawns, highlighting every movement, every shadow. She had no idea where the master's dogs would be at this time of night. Normally she was sleeping at this time, curled up in her bunk like a good little girl. But this good girl had had one thing too many taken from her.

She was going to get her spoon back.

Somehow, she had reached the edge of the kitchen. Pressing her back to the wall, she crept along under the eaves to the place where the water-butt stood underneath one of the smaller windows. Would she fit? She wasn't sure, but she knew that the latch was broken, and that she could pry it open with a little effort and hopefully no sound.

The spoon would be resting in the drawer with the rest of the silverware, where Doxie had put away countless other teaspoons just like it. But it wasn't like the other teaspoons. It was hers, and she wanted it back, no matter what it took, no matter what the risk.

That risk clawed at her belly like a live thing as she clambered up onto the water-butt. It was less full than she'd hoped, and it tilted horribly under her feet; she grabbed at the window, and it rocked for a heart-wrenching instant before thudding back onto its base with a wooden clunk. Doxie held her breath, clinging to the window, but there was no sound from inside the kitchen. Shaking uncontrollably, she managed to wiggle the window wide open. There was a burst of warmth from within the kitchen. Doxie pushed her head through, then one shoulder, and then - with a painful scrape along her skin - the other shoulder.

She placed her outstretched hands on the kitchen table, and with a little tumble and a painful blow to her knee, she was in the kitchen and slipping off the table onto the floor. Trembling, she cowered in the shadow of the table for a few heart-pounding moments. But there was no sound, no movement. Somehow, no one had heard her clumsy entrance.

She fixed her eyes on the grey outline of the scullery door. She only had to cross the floor, hurry a few yards into the scullery, pull open the drawer, and grab her spoon. She'd know it anywhere, even among a thousand other spoons of its like; it was so well-worn, so dear to her, so reverberating with the only connection she had to her past. It had become the focus of her world, and she felt herself moving across the floor almost involuntarily, as if magnetised to that last link with her identity.

Somehow, she was entering the dark scullery, and there was a slice of moonlight falling on the cabinet, gleaming on the brass knob of the drawer. Not daring to breathe, Doxie gripped the knob and slowly slid the drawer open as quietly as she could. There was only the tiniest of rattles. The moonlight flashed on silver. She looked down into a drawer full of teaspoons, gleaming silver on the black velvet, and she knew it the moment her eyes rested upon them.

Her spoon wasn't there.

Despair clutched at Doxie's lungs, refusing to let them expand and breathe. She felt as though she were drowning, as though the very air had turned to treacle. It had to be here. Why wasn't it here? Where else could it be? She grabbed at the spoons, reckless with shock, pawing them aside, ignoring the metallic clatter of their movement. It wasn't there. It was gone. She didn't know where it was. She didn't know where to find —

"Are you looking for this?"

Doxie whipped around and saw the last person she ever would have expected down here in the scullery. It was Celeste Roberts, the oldest of the Roberts' two unmarried daughters. The moonlight traced the soft curves of her face, her full lips, her dark eyes so filled with sorrow, her black hair caught up elegantly and piled on top of her head, its extravagance countering the utterly barren look in her eyes. Naked hope gleaned in them, desperate and afraid.

And in her hand, she held Doxie's spoon.

Doxie's eyes locked onto it. Even though she knew that Celeste's presence had to mean that she'd been caught — that she would be beaten, arrested, perhaps even hanged — she couldn't help but feel a tidal rush of relief at the sight. It had been her anchor for so long. She had been so lost without it.

Her heart filled with regret for Owen. She knew he'd be heartbroken, but she also had to have these answers, and so when she opened her mouth, it wasn't fear that came out. It was just lingering sorrow.

"Please," she said softly, "I just wanted to know my mama."

The spoon trembled in the woman's hand. Doxie's eyes found hers, and they were filling with tears. Again, she felt that strange pity for this woman she didn't know, this woman who had everything; but her eyes were empty—they were black seas of nothingness, of hollowness.

"Come with me," she croaked.

She left the kitchen, and Doxie couldn't seem to think of any other action but to follow. Stumbling after the tall, well-dressed figure, she felt like a sleepwalker dragged balloon-like in the wake of a dream. They left the scullery behind, and rose up a flight of stairs, and then another. Around Doxie, the house grew in grandeur, all sweeping staircases and statues in niches, paintings looming fiercely at them from the walls. Her feet sank deep into a rich carpet. Great, vaulted windows lurked behind thick drapes, and a fire burned warmly in every room. But Doxie barely noticed any of this. She was looking at the spoon, at the woman who drifted like a ghost in front of her, and she didn't know what any of this meant, but part of her expected the floor to melt under her feet and the whole world to spill into a spinning nightmare the way it had so often done back in the workhouse.

Yet the cold air on her face felt real when Celeste Roberts turned sharply left and pushed open a door that was dusty from disuse. They stepped into a large room, cold, and utterly dark. The darkness remained for a moment until Doxie heard a match scratching, and a candle was lit.

Fear struck her a little then when she saw Celeste Roberts' face. There were tears glittering on her cheeks, losing themselves in the wrinkles gathering at the corners of the woman's eyes.

"Please, ma'am." Doxie swallowed hard. "Where are we?"

She turned to Doxie, her eyes twin pits of pain. "Of course, you won't remember," she murmured. "But just... just look."

Obediently, Doxie turned, and saw the candlelight playing over a scene that haunted her with its familiarity. The carpet, navy blue underneath a film of dust. The vast hearth, with its bright rug. The shelves of books along the walls. The dolls lying on the floor.

And in the corner, all dapples and flowing black mane, the rocking-horse.

Celeste Roberts drifted over to the horse, running a hand over its smooth nose, its painted nostrils.

"He used to be mine, you know," she said. "I loved him better than any other toy. I was so looking forward to see... to see how my child loved him."

Doxie stared at Celeste, a thought forming in her mind, one that seemed too foolish to be true and yet too outlandish to be her imagination.

"But you're not married, ma'am," she said.

"That was the whole trouble." Celeste shook her head. "If we'd been married when my fiancé was killed in that terrible accident, when the brougham drove off the bridge and into the ditch..." Her voice shuddered. "I would have been a widow instead of a disgrace. I could have remarried. I could have kept..." She turned her face away.

Doxie's mouth felt very dry.

"You could have kept what?" she breathed.

Celeste was still staring down at the rocking-horse, caressing its mane, its velvet ears. Cold shudders crept up and down Doxie's spine in that dark room with the unspeaking woman.

Eventually, she said, "What's your name?"

"Ma'am, please." Doxie swallowed hard. "I…"

"Just tell me." Celeste's voice was different now, cold and hard and final.

There didn't seem to be anything else to do than to answer. "Doxie Shaw," Doxie breathed.

"Doxie…" Celeste sighed. "What a terrible name."

Doxie said nothing. Almost immediately, Celeste turned, and asked more. "How long have you been working at Apple Grove?"

The question and the coldness in Celeste's eyes caught Doxie off guard. "I… uh… six… six months? Four months?" She was panicking.

"Where did you work before that?" snapped Celeste.

"The w-workhouse," Doxie gulped.

"The workhouse!" Celeste's face crumpled a little, then strengthened. "When did you take this spoon?" she asked, yanking it from her dress and waving it in front of Doxie as she strode nearer to her, her eyes ablaze, as though she would strike her.

Doxie's words were a panicked squeal of fear. She had no idea what this erratic woman might do to her, but her eyes were terrifying.

"I didn't steal it!" she cried. "I didn't take it! It came with me! It was in my rags when they found me at the orphanage!" Sobs started to break up her words, tears cascading down her cheeks. "I don't know where it came from. I didn't mean for any trouble. I was only a baby." Her voice shattered, and she covered her face with her hands, crying with all of her heart. "I was only a baby," she breathed.

She was cowering, waiting for a blow of some kind from Celeste, but when the woman spoke, her voice was a grey wisp of what it had been a few seconds ago.

"Yes," she rasped. "You were only a baby."

Doxie lifted her head. Celeste's face was shattered in the moonlight, the lines of it crumpling and spreading across her smooth, white skin. She looked at Doxie, then at the spoon in her hands, and brought it gently to her chest as if to embrace something very small but very precious.

"Only a baby," she breathed, and her legs buckled under her. Celeste crumpled to the floor, sitting in a slumped heap, and her slender white shoulders began to tremble with sobs.

Doxie stared down at the woman, the spoon, the emblem. She looked around the nursery, her eyes resting on the dear old rocking-horse, and she knew it was true.

The sobbing grew quieter. Doxie looked down at the same moment that Celeste raised her head, and their eyes met, and something reached into the depths of Doxie's soul and spoke to her. And finally, after all these years, she knew.

Her voice almost failed her, but the word made it out anyway.

"Mama?" she breathed.

Fresh tears burst down Celeste's cheeks. She stretched out her arms, sobbing, smiling, weeping and laughing all at once.

"My daughter," she croaked. "My dear, dear daughter."

Her arms were waiting. It was the moment for which Doxie had spent her life hoping. She walked forward, at last, into her mother's embrace.

CHAPTER 23

A THOUSAND QUESTIONS spilled back and forth in the hansom-cab that rattled down the street, speeding further away from Apple Grove as dawn broke in the eastern sky. Neither Doxie nor Celeste had ever been in a cab before; Doxie had never even been in a horse-drawn carriage, but the novelty was lost on her. She was too busy gazing into Celeste's dark eyes, listening to her mother's story of all that had happened.

"I was only sixteen," Celeste was saying. "Sixteen — younger than you are now." She sighed. "Your father and I had been in love for two years, and we were engaged to be married. I let him... I let him go further than I really wanted to. I had just found out that I was pregnant when he was killed." She gave Doxie a wan smile. "It was an accident; a senseless freak accident, something that should never have happened. But then he was dead, and I didn't know what to do, so I said nothing. I couldn't keep the secret forever, of course. Mother was so furious when she noticed..." Her voice trailed off.

"I was right all along." Tears of joy were running down Doxie's cheek. "You wanted me after all."

"Of course, I wanted you. I had never really been loved before, and the moment I looked into your beautiful, beautiful eyes, I knew that you loved me and that I had never felt such love for anything before. You changed my life in one instant, my darling," said Celeste.

"You were everything I'd ever wanted, even though I hadn't known it. I wanted nothing in the world but to keep you. But my parents were adamant. They'd kept me under lock and key while I was expecting you, hidden me away to avoid shame on the family. They told me that if I wanted to keep you, I'd be thrown onto the streets. I would have chosen the streets over that house a thousand times. But you — you were so helpless."

Tears flooded from Celeste's eyes. "I couldn't do that to you, no matter how much I wanted you. So I took you to the orphanage. It all happened so quickly... there was no time for a note. But I seized a teaspoon from the tray, and I tucked it into your rags. I hoped that somehow it would lead you back to me."

She reached into her pockets again, pulling out the spoon and holding it out to Doxie.

Doxie didn't take it, not yet. She was too busy looking into her mother's eyes. "I'm so glad that it did," she whispered. "A part of me always knew you wanted me. Part of me could never rest until I found you."

"I haven't been whole without you, my daughter." Celeste smiled through her tears, her eyes truly shining.

Doxie glanced out of the window, at the lights speeding by, the day breaking. "Where... where are we going?" she asked.

It was the one thing they hadn't discussed back in the nursery. Celeste had been adamant that she wanted to leave Apple Grove, that she had tried time and time again to get her parents to look for her daughter, but they would never accept Doxie. Doxie didn't want to face them; she was happy to get away from that bleak manor house. And she was happy to be with Celeste. But now she feared Laurel Hall might be getting further and further away — and Owen with it.

"To a cottage," said Celeste. "My parents have been giving me an allowance for years, and I've put it all away in the bank. I always knew I wanted to get away from Apple Grove, and I always hoped you would come for me." She beamed. "A cousin of mine has a cottage tucked away in the back of a property he inherited just a couple of years ago. He's the only person who stood by me after you were born, who tried to help me find you, but he never could. Still, he said I could come and stay in the cottage whenever I found the courage to leave Apple Grove." She reached over, taking Doxie's hand. "I never found the courage, but I did find you, and you are enough."

Those three words were a balm upon Doxie's soul.

"How much further is it?" she asked.

"Oh, not far at all," said Celeste. "Laurel Hall is just down the road."

Laurel Hall! It was too beautiful to be true, and yet as the cab rattled up the driveway, Doxie saw familiar lights burning in the approaching stable yard, and she knew that all was going to be well. No matter what came next, all would truly be well.

They were driving over a humpbacked bridge now, the brook that ran down the bottom of the home paddock splashing beneath them, and Doxie's eyes fixed on the silver spoon. She held out her hand to Celeste. "May I have that, please?" she asked.

"Of course." Celeste gave it to her. "It's always been yours, my child."

Doxie pushed open the cab window and leaned out of it. The water flowed beneath the bridge, dark and rapid. Slowly, she held out the spoon, watched it shimmer one last time, and then let it fall.

"Why did you do that?" asked Celeste.

Doxie looked back at her, smiling, her heart too full for words.

"I don't need it anymore," she said.

There were a few seconds of silence as they gazed at one another, mother and daughter reunited at last.

"Can I ask you something?" said Doxie.

"Anything," said Celeste.

"What's my real name?" Doxie whispered.

Celeste smiled.

"Seraphine," she said. "You were my angel."

EPILOGUE

One Year Later

THE SNOW WAS FALLING THICKLY, powdering Owen's hat and scarf with perfect white diamonds. Seraphine couldn't take her eyes off him; off the flakes that sparkled on his long eyelashes, making his blue eyes shine more brightly than ever. Their fingers were entwined as they walked slowly up the cobbled path leading up to the front door of the cottage, but they didn't say anything. Nothing needed to be said. The joyous silence between them, quivering with sheer happiness, was more than enough.

Wrapped in this silence, they reached the front step of the cottage and paused to face one another. There was nothing more perfect than the look in Owen's eyes, the love with which they roamed over Seraphine's face, as though he were committing it to memory, imprinting it irrevocably in his tender heart.

"I'll see you tomorrow morning," Owen murmured.

"I wish you didn't have to go back to the loft," Seraphine sighed. She leaned against him a little. "I wish you could stay here with me."

"Someday, my love," said Owen. "I wish you could spend your days tending a home of our own, a family..." His voice trailed off. "I wish you didn't have to work at Laurel Hall as a nurse."

"I love the children." Seraphine beamed.

"I know you do." Owen kissed her forehead. "Still, I keep hoping for the day we finally have the money to marry."

"It'll come." Seraphine took his hand and squeezed it. "I know it will. And then it'll help Mama, too. I'm worried about what will happen when her savings run out..."

"We'll take care of her." Owen smiled. "I promise."

"Thank you," said Seraphine. "You know what she means to me." She pushed open the door. "Won't you come in and warm yourself by the fire, just for a few moments before you walk back to the stables?"

"Of course." Owen laughed. "How could I refuse?"

They stepped into the cosy cottage that was Seraphine's dream come true: a home where she lived at last with the mother who had always loved her. Even though Mama had none of the finery she'd enjoyed at Apple Grove, she was still happy here, far happier than she'd ever been before.

Normally this was the case, at least. When Owen and Seraphine stepped into the kitchen now, a thrill of shock ran through Seraphine's body. Mama was sitting at the kitchen table, staring down at a letter that lay before her, and her face was ashen.

"Mama!" Seraphine ran to her side. "What is it?"

Mama looked up at her, and her eyes filled with tears. "Oh, my love, I can't believe it," she cried.

"You can't believe what?" Seraphine gasped, rushing to her and wrapping her arms around her. "What's happened?"

"It's your grandparents," sobbed Mama.

Seraphine's heart hurt. "Oh, Mama," she said. "They're still not accepting us, are they?"

"No. They're not. But a solicitor just came." Mama gazed up at Seraphine, grinning in bewilderment. "Sera, they're paying me my inheritance."

The words hung in the kitchen for a few long moments.

"They're what?" gasped Owen.

Mama grinned. "Owen," she said, "how would you like to own your own livery?"

Owen's eyes began to gleam. "Celeste..." he began.

"It's more than enough. More than enough!" Mama laughed, leaping to her feet. "We can start your livery, and we'll be able to give Seraphine a real education, and we'll never have to worry about money again – and oh – oh, you two can finally be married!"

Seraphine felt as though her heart would explode from pure happiness. She turned to Owen, and his eyes were alight.

"Seraphine," he gasped. "We can have our own home."

The old song, the one she'd always sung as a lullaby, ran through her mind again. She had finally learned the last stanza.

An exile from home splendour dazzles in vain

Oh, give me my lowly thatched cottage again

The birds singing gaily that came at my call

And gave me the peace of mind dearer than all

Home, home, sweet, sweet home

There's no place like home, there's no place like home!

"Oh, Owen," she whispered, her eyes filling with tears at the thought of their future together, of soothing their own child with that song. "You have always been my home."

The End

CONTINUE READING...

THANK you for reading **The Orphan's Silver Spoon! Are you wondering what to read next?** Why not read **The Fishmonger's Daughter? Here's a sneak peek for you:**

Abbie Hughes kept a wary eye on the brass-buttoned bobby on the street corner. It seemed as though he hadn't seen them yet; he was busy grasping the collar of a grubby, out-at-the-elbows character who had pinched some of the half-wilted peaches right out of the grocer's window. Abbie could imagine how hungry the man must have been to steal from the grocer. She knew that hunger well – it gnawed at her own belly right now. She knew that desperation, and she had felt dismay when the grocer had shouted, "Stop! Thief!" and the clanging bell of the bobby had sounded around the corner.

One thing that was for sure—the policeman was deeply occupied in bellowing at the man, and he wasn't paying any attention to Abbie.

"We should go," hissed her little sister at her elbow. "While he's busy – before he sees us."

Abbie wasn't sure what it was about their tiny, grubby stand that made them such a target. If it wasn't the police chasing them off for being a public menace (presumably it was very menacing to sell thin bone broth to gaunt, grubby people), it was the nearby shopkeepers who didn't like their dirty faces and unwashed clothes detracting from the appearance of the street. But she knew she and Gail could get the stand packed up in a matter of seconds if they had to.

"Come on, Abbie," said Gail. Gail's eyes were wide and round in her pinched, dirty face, making her look older than her twelve years.

Abbie looked back at the line of people waiting silently for soup. Several of them had melted away at the appearance of the policeman, but a few remained, hopefully clutching their bowls and pennies. The pennies gleamed a little in the fading evening light. Abbie was acutely aware of how much her family needed them.

"Quick," she hissed, gesturing at the next customer.

The old man shuffled over to her, dropped a few pennies in her hand and passed her the bowl. Gail stared at Abbie, the ladle clutched in her hand. It had a broken handle. "Are you sure?"

"Hurry, Gail," said Abbie.

Gail shrugged and started spooning the watery mixture into the bowl. It wasn't much; a pale, oily substance, made from whatever tiny scraps of meat were left on the bones Abbie bought from the butcher, and maybe one or two wilted turnips if she could get them. But it was piping hot thanks to the wood fire crackling under the great old iron pot. The old man's eyes widened in glee as he wrapped his hands, encased in fingerless gloves, around the bowl.

"Next," hissed Abbie, shooting a glance at the policeman. He was binding the wrists of the thief, the grocer looking on with great contentment.

Click Here to Continue Reading!

https://www.ticahousepublishing.com/victorian-romance.html

THANKS FOR READING

I<small>F YOU LOVE</small> V<small>ICTORIAN</small> R<small>OMANCE,</small> **Click Here**

https://victorian.subscribemenow.com/

to hear about all **New Faye Godwin Romance Releases! I will let you know as soon as they become available!**

Thank you, Friends! If you enjoyed ***The Orphan's Silver Spoon,*** would you kindly take a couple minutes to leave a positive review on Amazon? It only takes a moment, and positive reviews truly make a difference. Thank you so much! I appreciate it!

Much love,

Faye Godwin

MORE FAYE GODWIN VICTORIAN ROMANCES!

We love rich, dramatic Victorian Romances and have a library of Faye Godwin titles just for you! (Remember that ALL of Faye's Victorian titles can be downloaded FREE with Kindle Unlimited!)

CLICK HERE to discover Faye's Complete Collection of Victorian Romance!

https://ticahousepublishing.com/victorian-romance.html

ABOUT THE AUTHOR

Faye Godwin has been fascinated with Victorian Romance since she was a teen. After reading every Victorian Romance in her public library, she decided to start writing them herself —which she's been doing ever since. Faye lives with her husband and young son in England. She loves to travel throughout her country, dreaming up new plots for her romances. She's delighted to join the Tica House Publishing family and looks forward to getting to know her readers.

contact@ticahousepublishing.com

Printed in Great Britain
by Amazon